A LESSON IN MAGIC

by Amanda Huxley

A Prequel

THE MAGISTOWE ACADEMY SAGA

A Mightier Than the Sword UK Publication

©2023

MAGISTOWE ACADEMY SAGA: A LESSON IN MAGIC

A Lesson in Magic

Magistowe Academy Saga

By Amanda Huxley

A Mightier Than the Sword UK Publication

Paperback Edition

ISBN Kindle 978-1-7385919-2-3

ISBN Paperback 978-1-99-117192-4

Chapter 1

In a small village, high up in the mountains, a small family had always enjoyed living a quiet and simple life.

They were not particularly wealthy, nor remarkable in any way. They lived a peaceful existence that most would consider idyllic.

Even the family dynamic fitted with the perfect ideal - a mother, a father and a daughter.

The father herded sheep during the summer, and in the winter he helped by doing odd jobs around the village. For decades his family had lived in the village. His father had done the same as him, and his father before him, in a way, he had gone into the family business.

His wife had been born in the village as well. Her family had not been there as long as his, but they were well respected, and hard working.

She made clothes all year round. Nothing too fancy. But enough that people would come to her when they were ready to buy something, or they needed to have something repaired.

The daughter was an unremarkable creature. She was not clever, and she was not what you would necessarily call pretty either.

She had a way with animals, but no talent for sewing. Nobody knew what exactly she would make herself as she grew up. Some even believed that nothing would come of her, and she would be humoured with small jobs by those in the village, enough to feed and clothe herself, but she would never amount to more than she was now.

The village was found on the side of a mountain, with tall pine trees growing in a vast forest above it. Below it were fertile fields that spread out as far as the eyes could see and the farms that lay outside the village were as much a part of the community as those that lived at the heart of the small cluster of cottages and huts.

It had been many decades since wolves had been seen near this village. The wolves lived in the depths of the forest and had no reason to venture out of the trees whilst the game within the forest was plentiful.

It did not mean from time to time that they were not seen, though these sightings were rare and often at a distance.

But after one particularly dry summer, and a very harsh winter, the deer had fled from the forest in search of food and water further afield. The wolves were starving, much like those in the village, and when the wolves began to roam beyond the trees, there was tragedy.

The man and his wife were found dead in their home and the daughter was found hidden under the floorboards alive, but traumatised.

It was the wolves that were blamed for it, but the girl has seen everything and she knew full well that it was not wolves that had killed her family.

It was a beast that walked on its hind legs, a hulking creature of impressive strength and intelligence. It had managed to unlock the door to their home from the outside.

The moment that the lock had begun to scrape, her parents had pushed back the sheepskin on the floor, and opened the hatch to the small cellar below, bundling their daughter down into it before closing it again.

There had been no time to replace the rug, but when the beast had entered, it had laughed.

"I am not here for the child," it said. It was there for her parents and it took her almost as easily. The screams of her parents as they had been murdered had rung in the girl's ears, and she knew that she would never forget those terrible sounds.

She had screwed up her eyes tight and covered her ears, but her hands were not able to block out the sounds.

From the time of her parents death, there was some little money for her to live on in the village. But she had no trade, and there was no way for her to earn money of her own. Villagers began to talk about whether they should take the poor girl in, feed her, clothe and look after her. At least help her to find her place in the world.

But every time any of them tried to approach her she would beg them to go look for the monster that had killed her parents. Beg them to follow her wild stories into grave danger, and when it became clear to the villages that she would not stop for these outrageous tales, their willingness to help her melted away.

They began to resent her, and claiming her cursed, claiming her mind had been stolen and would never be returned, they cast her from the village.

What precious few things she owned, the girl could carry, but it was not much. She had a cloak that her mother had made for her no matter how cold it was or how badly the wind bit, she was never called when she wore this cloak.

Her mother used to say while she wore that cloak, that she was protected by her mother's love; protected from all harm and that only harm would be able to touch her on her feet.

But her father had seen to that. He had made shoes for her feet, in a fashion, from the wool of the sheep that he looked after.

The leather on the outside was cold to touch but fleece lined inside making them warm and comfortable.

Somehow water never seemed to seep into them and her feet were always dry no matter how deep through a snow bank she trudged.

Her mother used to say that it was her father's love protecting her, and the girl often wondered why her parents would say such things.

After all, none of the other children in the village had parents who said such things. But then she had always considered her parents to be quite different to all the other parents she had met.

That was all she had that was worth taking from her home. She only had one dress and there was very little food that remained.

Anything else that was small enough to fit in the bundle she carried was thrown in alongside the food and the only nightgown she owned.

She was escorted to the edge of the village by a jeering mob, and two of them remained at the edge of the village to ensure she did not try to return to the house.

She watched from the edge of the village as her home was boarded up and a bar was placed upon the door. A home left abandoned to ruin.

She felt that she was betraying her mother and father as she left the village, leaving them behind with these cold people who did not care for them, but at the same time she had no choice.

They were buried alongside their parents and

their grandparents. But though she had been born in this village, she would not die there.

She hoped that her parents would understand why she had to leave, even though she had no idea what she was going to do with her life.

The first thought that came to her was the thought of revenge. Seeking out whatever it was that had killed her parents, and taking it upon herself to kill it for their sake. But as it had killed her parents so easily, she knew without help that she herself would suffer the same fate.

She made her way out of the farmland that belonged to the village and walked along the tree line of the great forest that surrounded it.

She knew better than to wander too deep into the forest alone, but her father had taught her the paths to take to get through the thinnest part of the forest. She knew a chant that her mother had taught her to ward off bears and other dangerous animals.

She had seen her mother use the chant to cause

wolves to run from the pastures and protect the sheep. She did not know how it worked, but she was glad that she knew it.

There was only a small amount of food that she had brought as there had not been much food in the house. She knew that it would not last long, and after it was gone, she did not know what she would do.

All she could do was walk.

She walked for five days through the trees. On the first day she found a river and decided to follow it. Water was a good sign. Animals would come to drink from it and she hoped that there would be a village or some living further downstream.

She did find some animals but she did not know how to hunt them. She found some berries but she did not know if they were safe to eat. On the fifth day, the river became a trickle, and then it disappeared altogether.

She did not know how far she had come or how she would get back as she had lost all sight of where she had come from.

Without water, she knew that she would not last long. Her food was all gone and now she had nothing to drink. She searched for two days, trying to find her way back to the river, but she could not, and soon she was so completely lost that she had no hope of ever leaving the trees.

She sat down on the ground a closed her eyes. She had nothing left but to try and sleep and hope that she died quickly.

No one in the village would ever know what had become of her, nor, she thought, would they care. Lying on the forest floor, she screwed up her eyes and began to cry; whispering apologies to her parents for failing them.

As she lay there, sobbing, she heard a faint sound. It was coming from somewhere nearby, just through a small stand of trees. She dried her eyes and got to her feet, intrigued by the sound.

As she followed it, the sound grew louder until

she found herself in front of a cave. No light came from inside of it but the sound definitely originated from its depths.

As she stood there, staring into the black, she thought she heard her mother's voice calling out to her.

"Stop crying, child," it said.

She shook her head and tried to block the sound out of her mind. It was impossible her mother was calling to her. She was dead and there was nothing that could bring her back.

"Come into the cave," her father's voice called out.

Hearing both of her parents' voices, she was certain that she was close to death and they beckoning her to join them in the afterlife. She felt scared as she took what she thought was her last deep breath and stepped into the cave.

With one hand on the wall she slowly walked into the gloom. She expected the darkness to overwhelm her, to swallow her whole and for her soul to be transported from this plane to the next. But the further she went into the cave, the lighter it became.

The light was not the white light of day, but dancing violet and blue light that she had seen in the nights sky before.

The light was warm and inviting, and not at all what she had been expecting to find. She kept moving, the light getting brighter until she found herself in a large round cavern. In the centre of the cavern was the source of the light.

A pool of clear water, with a fountain at the centre, seemed to be where the light was coming from. The water was cleaner than she had ever seen and she could not help but run to the pool.

She knelt down beside the water's edge and began to drink deeply from the pool. There were other wonders in the cavern to behold, but her only thoughts were about survival, and the treasures within a single room meant nothing to her.

When she had drunk all she could be collapsed back on the floor. The sweet tasting water had saved her for the moment, but now she was out of immediate danger, she wondered where she was.

It was only then that she began to take in the room, the light and the many treasures that filled the natural alcoves in the wall.

"Oh good, I am so glad you found your way here," a familiar voice echoed around the chamber, but there was no one there. The girl thought for a moment that she was losing her mind and it was all an elaborate hallucination; that really she was lying the forest somewhere, close to death.

"Peace, peace, you are not in danger. You are of sound mind. We did not know if you would hear us, if you would follow our voices, but you are here!" another familiar voice said.

In the light of the fountain, the figures of her parents appeared before her eyes.

"What are you doing here?" the girl stammered,

unsure she could believe what she was seeing.

"We are here because of you," her mother smiled.

"How are you here now?" the girl asked with confusion.

"We are here now because we chose to come here to help you find your way," her father replied.

"What are you talking about? I don't understand any of this," the girl said, clutching her head.

"It is all right. You will soon enough. This is the wellspring of magic, and both your father and I drank from it much the same age as you. As our parents before us, and your grandparents and grandparents did. For generations our families have travelled her to drink and pass on the secrets of ancient magic. We were getting ready to bring you here, to show you this place, to tell you all you needed to know to find your way in the world," her mother explained.

"But before we could, the enemy found us. As

you had not drunk and would not know of anything of the world beyond the village, the enemy let you live," her father continued.

"We understand time is short, and there is much we must tell you. The name you're given at your birth, or at least the one you know yourself as is not your true name," her mother said.

"What is my name then?" the girl asked.

"That is up to you to discover. You will hear your name whisper to you when you're ready to hear it. Your heart, now one with magic, will tell you. It might take lounger for you to hear it than others before you because of all you have been through, and because you need to hide from the enemy for a time," her father said seriously.

"Who is this enemy? What does he want? Why stop you?" the girl asked, her head was swimming and she was not sure how much lounger she could stay awake.

"For now, the less you know, the more

protected you shall be. What I will say is that the enemy has been at work for many centuries, trying to remove magic from this world. We took you to hide in the village, to keep you safe from him as you have a great destiny to fulfil. The shoes and cloak that we made for you, we filled with our magic, and our love. Whilst you wear them both, the enemy will not be able to find you. At least for now," her father said.

"Their protection will not last forever, but you are safe within this cavern. Sleep and we will come back to you when you have rested," her mother soothed.

"Time is short, but we will do all we can before we have to leave you. You possess powers from the fountain, they have awakened within you. Simply think about what it is you want, and it shall appear. But know this, your magic will not allow you to summon those back from the dead. Souls must pass beyond the veil and cannot be retrieved. Those that raise the dead raise corpses that hunger for souls something they can never possess," her father warned.

"Gold summoned through magic is also cursed. Greed only leads to dark powers and it is the sole driving desire of our enemy. But to summon food you wish to eat is not greed. Summon it and it will stay as long as you want it to," her mother moved forward and gently kissed her daughter on the forehead.

The girl nodded and closed her eyes and focused on the bed from her bedroom.

She held up her hands and felt something strange in the tips of her finger and a warmth coming from them. A moment later she opened her eyes and was so surprised to see her bed before her. She gasped and fell over in backwards into the fountain.

"Wasn't that easy?" her father said. She nodded as she climbed into the bed. She closed her eyes and thought of how cold she was and a fire appeared close to her bed, instantly.

She soon drifted off to sleep in the warmth and comfort of her bed. Her mother watched her from the fountain. There were a great many things that would be needed, but for now rest was the most important thing.

As the girl slept, her parents magically showed her images throughout the night - all those who had come before her and the many battles fought with the enemy.

When the girl awoke, she was hungry and conjured some bread, cheese and an apple as well as a glass of milk to drink.

Her parents waited patiently for her to finish eating and then urged her to rest again. The more she slept, the more they could share of the past without having to explain the details or overwhelming her.

She woke, ate and then slept again for three days, and by the time the three days had ended, the girl knew all that had happened to those that had come before.

"Now you are ready to learn," her father said.

Chapter 2

It did not take her long to learn the fundamental abilities of magic. She became quite adept at using her imagination to think things into existence. But her abilities soon went far beyond that.

Far beyond the existence of simple items of rudimentary design.

Under the tutelage of the spirits of her mother and father she began to understand her magic and its place in the world. How it held things together and provided a bridge between reality and the imagination.

The more she practised, the more nuanced and refined her creations became as well. She did not realise that the purity of her magic could easily be corrupted and used for more nefarious purposes. She had no desires for power or greed. Her anger at those who had exiled her from her home and vanished in the face of her parents and her new abilities.

She did not see how destructive her abilities could be or how important it was for her to be able to control her abilities before she left the wellspring.

Months had passed in the blink of an eye and her mother's presence was now growing weaker by the day.

"Before our time together is at an end, my child, I must tell you of all the different types of magic in this world. There are many different disciplines, but all branches of magic stem from a single source. They all come from the ancient magic you now know. All magic exists as part of a whole, the other magics could all fade out of existence, but as long as the ancient magic exists, magic will endure and renew itself. But if the ancient magic is lost, then all other magic will cease to be as well."

"Can I learn these other magics as well?" the girl asked hopefully.

"Sadly not. You are what is called a conduit. Through you, others have access to magic. Through your magic, others can find their path and place in this world. But though your heart is pure and your magic is only for the good of all, you cannot control what others might use it for. Magic can be used for evil as well as good, and there are those who have been so hurt by evil, or have had their hearts twisted by jealousy, that they wish to see magic disappear from this world entirely. There are those who would also wish to see the good of magic gone and only the evil remain. Those who wish to destroy magic and those that wish to corrupt it shall seek you all their lives, you and the wellspring," her mother's spirit explained.

"Is that why you and father died? Because I am the conduit?" the girl asked with a tearful sob catching in her throat.

"No, my child, that is not why we died. I was the conduit and your father was my guardian. When I died, the role became yours to fulfil. Do not believe any who say that you were the cause of our demise," her mother said softly.

"Does that mean I need a guardian?" the girl asked.

"It does, but you do not need to search for a guardian. Your guardian will find you when the time is right. Just as your father found me," her mother smiled sadly.

"And what about the darkness that took you from me?" the girl asked tearfully. "What do I do about?"

"The darkness will find you as well. He is searching for this place constantly, but he cannot find it. The wellspring cannot due to a curse cast upon him, as long as the wellspring does not wish to be found by him it shall remain hidden from his eyes. But he feels that if he tries for long enough, if he perseveres enough and kills everyone that is chosen by magic that the wellspring will eventually relent and choose him to be the conduit instead. He has lived far lounger than any natural being should, his life augmented by corrupting the magic that flows through us for his own selfish gain. It has made him into a creature without soul, without compassion, and without love. Whilst you are within the walls of the wellspring, you are safe. He cannot find or harm you here," her mother said with a sad smile.

"But?" the girl asked.

"But you cannot stay in this place forever either. You are needed out in the world," her mother sighed.

"Then what must I do to stay hidden from him?" the girl asked.

"You must choose a name, a name that the world can know you by. Your name shall be your protection. The name we gave you is not your true name but a mirror, a glass of protection. You shall find your true name in time, but when you do, share it with no one else. To know your true name gives others power over you. Even your guardian should not know it. For now, you must choose a name to protect yourself," her mother said warningly.

The girl thought for a moment.

"I have a name. My name is Riley," the girl said firmly.

"Riley what?" her mother asked her patiently

"Riley Sonnen," the girl said decidedly.

"Well then, Riley Sonnen, now that you have your name it is time for you to begin your life outside of these walls. When a child comes of age, they must decide what their future path is, what they shall make their life's work, where all their energy shall be focused every single day of their lives. You are not of any age to be forced to finding your way in the world, but that there is nothing that we can do to change that now. Your father will come to you again, one final time to speak with you on this, but this is the last time we shall meet," her mother smiled down at her daughter.

"No mother, stay," Riley begged.

"I cannot, child. My time has passed. I have taught you all I can. I wish I could have stayed with you, inspired and protected you. I wanted you to have a life of love and laughter far from the the responsibilities you now must bear," her mother said and closed her eyes. Her form was growing fainter in the glow of the wellspring.

"What if I make the wrong choice? What if I make a bad decision? What if I choose the wrong path and waste the magic?" Riley sounded terrified as she watched her mother fading before her.

"Life is full of wrong choices, bad decisions and wasted opportunities. There is no possible way that you can avoid them. Set yourself a goal and keep moving towards it, no matter what missteps you might make, no matter what obstacles may fall in your path. You shall find a way, I know you shall," her mother said warmly.

"What if I fail?" Riley asked quietly.

"Then at least you will have tried," her mother replied. "I love you little one, and no matter what happens in your life, that will never change. Goodbye child, I shall see you again in a world without death and end," her mother said as she faded away to nothing.

"Mother, no!" Riley cried out and reached to try and stop her mother from vanishing, but it was too late. The girl could not stop the tears that tumbled forth from her eyes and collapsed on her knees in front of the wellspring.

"Do not weep child, she has passed to a peaceful place, a place without pain or sorrow," her father said kindly. "I will join her there soon, but before I leave you, I am here to guide you in your final decision. What is it that you wish to do with your life?"

Riley closed her eyes to stop the tears and focus her thoughts.

"I want to help people. I want to help those like me, and like mother. Those who use magic, those who are exiled from their homes, those that live in fear, and those that have no other place in the world," Riley said after she had thought for a while.

"Very good. Now sit, meditate, listen to the wellspring. Let the magic come to you, let it flow through you. Let it guide you on the steams and eddies into the heart of the wellspring. Let yourself become completely attuned to it, set aside all else and know only magic. Let it show you the path to tread, the very depths of your heart and soul, let it open your mind to new thoughts, ideas and possibilities, and when you have reached the point where you are ready, the wellspring will put you where you are meant to be to carry out whatever tasks lay before you," her father instructed.

"Will you be here still?" Riley asked tentatively.

"I shall not. I must go to your mother's side. I shall watch over you until this is done, I will guard you as I have guarded her. But before you begin, know that I shall always be proud to have called you my daughter," her father said with a smile.

"Thank you, father," Riley said and took a deep breath. She sat down and crossed her legs, and closed her eyes.

"Good, now focus on each breath, one in, one

out, good, now let the wellspring speak," her father said.

Riley focused on her breath, all other thoughts were banished from her mind. Then she felt it, a tugging in her soul a calling to follow a blue ribbon in her mind.

The ribbon twirled about her, causing her to dance and leap, spin and laugh as it pulled her along with it. Around her body the wind began to rise. It began as gentle breeze at first but then it grew to great gusts as the magic lifted her from the floor.

But Riley did not feel it, her mind was lost in the wellspring, her heart and soul were diving deeper into the magical torrents learning new and greater secrets whilst her mind danced with joy as it followed the blue ribbon.

Days passed as Riley was transformed by the wellspring, and her father stood watch. Four days and three nights went by until he faded from sight and Riley was lifted from the wellspring cave.

When she opened her eyes she found herself on a hillside overlooking a vast and empty landscape. Beneath her feet she could feel the pulse of the wellspring close by but where it was exactly she could not say.

She stood upon the hillside and knew the task that lay before her, but more importantly, she knew her true name.

CHAPTER 3

The land had no one living on it, and no one to claim it. There was no lord who collected taxes. It was a wasteland of scrub that was of no use to farmer, king, merchant or craftsman.

The only one who could find the land of any use was Riley. The wellspring had chosen her the perfect place to begin. She could feel the power of the ancient magic was strong under her feet and decided to begin small.

She imagined a home for herself, one made from stone with five rooms. She imagined a kitchen, a library filled with books, a room to sleep in, a porch to sit upon and watch the horizon, a room to eat and a room in which to practice her magic away from prying eyes.

When the magic was woven, before her stood a

house bigger than she had ever seen in her life. Not even the most important members of the village she had been exiled from had homes of such a size.

She imagined a garden of flowers that she could sit and look at in the evening in front of the porch. Around the back of the house she imagined vegetable plants growing, some chickens, some sheep and a cow.

Next she used her magic to create a chicken coop and barn for the animals to sleep in and a fence to keep the animals away from her vegetables.

Though she had never raised animals or grown anything herself, she had spent her life around those that did and she had learned a great deal about farming and agriculture.

The first week of life in the wasteland was simple, quiet and followed a routine built around growing food and caring for the animals whilst she used her magic to create her meals, the water and the feed for the animals.

On the 8th day a figure appeared at her door. To

begin with, Riley was frightened by the sound of knocking on her door, but she knew that if she was to build a community on this land, she would eventually have to find others to join it.

When she opened the door, an old man was stood there clutching a staff. He looked to be at least seventy years old and had lived a hard life. His hands were covered with scratches, his face was a patchwork of bruises and his teeth were broken and crooked.

"Excuse me, young woman, but what is this land?" he croaked.

"A beginning," Riley replied.

"A beginning for what?" the man asked.

"A beginning of a place I hope that will provide safety for all those who are misunderstood," Riley said slowly.

"A noble goal. Did you build this magnificent house?" he asked as he stepped back from the door to appreciate the building.

"I did," Riley said slowly.

"I see. Then you are the one," he said with an element of satisfaction. He looked Riley up and down and nodded his head with slight approval.

"I don't know what you mean," Riley said and moved to close the door.

"Please, I am not in league with the darkness. My name is Cornelius. I am an enchanter and conjurer, I once knew a woman named Adele and her guardian, Godfrey. I know the darkness found them, but their daughter survived. I believe that you are their child. Am I correct?" Cornelius asked hopefully.

"My parents were Adele and Godfrey, and they were taken by the darkness," Riley confirmed.

"Then you are the one that the wellspring has chosen; and you wish to build a community to protect others. You really are as unique as your mother said," Cornelius chuckled to himself.

"Why did you come here?" Riley asked.

"I came because the wellspring bid me to. I have been searching for you since I felt the absence of your parents from this world. I am sorry that I was not able to help them against the darkness, but as you can tell from my appearance, the darkness has been trying to prevent me from accomplishing my mission," Cornelius explained.

"Then you came here to help me?" Riley asked nervously.

"I did indeed. If you would be willing to share a meal out in this lovely garden we can talk of your plans, such as they are, and see what we should do next," Cornelius suggested.

He stood in her garden, and with a great deal of effort, he placed his staff in front of himself and began uttering an incantation. As he muttered, the wind began to move around them and a table with two chairs and piled high with food appeared before them both.

"Come sit," Cornelius said brightly. "Though I cannot create in the same way that you can, I am not without talent."

"You know about other branches of magic?" Riley asked with wonder.

"I do. Come, sit and eat and we can make plans for the future," Cornelius encouraged her warmly.

The two talked for hours until the sun began to sink from the sky. Riley was not certain about inviting the man into her home, but she did not need to worry.

"Could you, perhaps, create for me a modest house? A place with a bed, a hearth and a place for me to perfect my enchantments?" Cornelius asked. "After all, if the community is to grow, then we shall need places for people to live."

Riley grinned and nodded enthusiastically. She imagined a house that she thought would be perfect for the old man. She placed it opposite her own with a front garden that he could sit and eat it.

She gave him a bedroom, a room for enchanting and a kitchen. When she was done, she opened her eyes to find Cornelius grinning at her in wonder.

"It is magnificent, far grander than I deserve,

child. I thank you for the very depths of my soul," Cornelius said, his voice cracking with emotion.

"You are welcome. In the morning, we should begin our plans to build," Riley said and the pair said goodnight.

Riley did not know what the community would need, she had no experience in planning or building, but Cornelius knew all that would be needed.

"First we shall need two castles, grand and towering structures that stand at the centre of the community. There must be enough space around them to grow and chance as our needs dictate, but they are the central point that all else can be build around," Cornelius said.

The pair walked to the centre of the wasteland to begin construction on the two castles. A great deal of time and effort was required to build the two great structures, and though Cornelius was able to help a little, it was up to Riley to use her magic to bring the two castles into being.

They were not meant to be homes, but both had grand kitchens with large fires capable of providing food for huge numbers of people.

Once the castles came into being, Riley created a river that ran alongside the two buildings. Next came roads and bridges, then buildings for shops and craftsmen to inhabit, a large forge was brought into existence, and place for the brewing of potions.

Cornelius soon found that he was more useful tending to the garden and animals than he was trying to help Riley with her magic.

Four months after they began the construction, a group of travellers happened upon the city, refugees fleeing persecution due to their magical gifts. Cornelius welcomed them all and introduced them to Riley as the leader of the community.

Then more people came, and word soon spread of a place that those with magic could call home with others of their kind. It soon became clear that one of the castles was to be the cultural centre and where the

the leaders of the community would meet and discuss the running and day-to-day business of such a large place. The other castle was to become the school where magical and non-magical people could be educated as well as learn more about magic.

As word spread, it was not only humans that came to the community, but magical creatures came seeking sanctuary. Some of the creatures were at home amongst the people and bustle streets of the community, whereas others needed their own habitats to thrive.

Riley created all that was needed for the community to grow and for all those that came to find a place where they could belong.

When the majority of the infrastructure was in place, and there were enough non-magical people in the community to take on the jobs of construction and maintenance as well as farming, Riley was free to lead the community and finally name the refuge she had created.

Magistowe.

CHAPTER 4

Rumours of Magistowe soon spread throughout the many kingdoms that bordered the wasteland. None of the kingdoms had ever laid claim to the scrub as it seemed to be of no value to them, but it bordered every one of them.

So when a magical stronghold filled with all those that had been chased out of the kingdoms grew suddenly in the middle of worthless into a prosperous, independent nation, the kings and peasants alike were worried.

To them it was a shadow of fear cast wide and far, and all of the kings agreed that Magistowe was a threat to the stability and safety of their nations.

The largest of those nations was ruled by King Ruettigur. He was a powerful man, but a fair one for the most part. His subjects respected him, but it was his Knight-Marshal who was loved by the people.

Berengar Wolf was the son of a lesser house of nobles, but his dedication to duty, his skills in combat, a wise head on his shoulders, and the care he showed to all the people of his nation had allowed him to rise to one of the most powerful positions in the land.

His notoriety and elevated rank had not corrupted his character. He was the same kind, patient and dedicated individual that he had been as a child and young recruit.

When fear of Magistowe spread, it was to King Ruettigur that the other monarchs looked for help and protection. It was to Berengar Wolf that the king turned to for a solution.

The king decreed that an army be raised to take the kingdom by force, but Berengar suggested that all out war was not the way for this situation to be resolved and that sending an envoy to Magistowe would not only help determine if they were a threat to the other kingdoms, but perhaps even forge an alliance with them.

King Ruettigur thought for a long time before he agree that he would send an envoy to Magistowe to speak with them before declaring war.

Prince Cynfael, Ruettigur's eldest son and heir, was chosen as the envoy and Berengar was given the task of protecting the prince with a small retinue of soldiers on the mission.

They set out on their mission amidst pouring rain with no fanfare or grandeur. They rode under the banners of the kingdom and a white flag of parley.

The sorcerers knew that the party was coming to their lands long before the envoys reached their border.

A group of centaurs, minotaurs, griffins, minokawas, wyverns, chimeras, fauns, dryads, longma, chollima, and shapeshifters all lined the route the envoys part took into the lands of Magistowe.

It was a show of their force borne of fear. To the magical and mythical creatures that now called Magistowe home, the royalty and soldiers of other lands were the embodiment of those that had driven them out of their homes, persecuted them, hunted them, and forced them into exile. In the borders of the magical sanctuary they had thrived and felt protected, and would now return the favour and protect their new home from any threat the envoys brought with them.

Prince Cynfael was unnerved by seeing so many dangerous and deadly creatures in such numbers watching them arrive, but Berengar kept his men calm and showed deference and respect to them all as they passed. He did not stare straight ahead, but made eye contact and bowed his head in greeting to the creatures as they made their way towards the central city.

With the number of people and creatures that had come to Magistowe, there were now settlements across the land. Trade within the nation was thriving and even some merchants from the neighbouring lands travelled to do business with the magical civilisation.

When the envoy group reached one of the outlying towns that skirted the great city, a group of sorcerers was waiting to greet them.

The envoys were taken to the town hall and given a feast and beds to rest in after their long journey. The prince was nervous and did not sleep, despite the warmth of the welcome. Berengar was the only one of his men who had an even remotely restful night.

The following morning, the envoy were given an escort to the heart of the Magistowe lands where the doors of the sorcerers' tower, one of the two castles at the centre of the city, were open to them.

It has been ten years since Riley had found the wellspring, ten years of building and growing a place where all people could be safe.

Riley had blossomed into a beautiful young woman with raven hair and startling blue eyes. She stood at the head of a group of five sorcerers that were waiting to welcome the envoys on the steps of the sorcerers' tower.

She wore flowing purple robes and her hair was pinned back with golden flower pins that glinted in the sunlight.

Cornelius was stood on her right, dressed in black and leaning on his staff for support.

"Welcome to Magistowe, prince of Ruettigur's lands. We have been expecting you. We hope that your journey through our lands has been a safe and hospitable one. My name is Riley Sonnen, and I am the leader of our fair community. These ladies and gentlemen are the council who support me in overseeing the safety and prosperity of this place, introductions can be made when we are all seated inside," Riley said with a smile.

"Your welcome is most appreciated, Riley, first of her land. My name is Cynfael, and this is Berengar, Knight-Marshal of my father's army. Your people and their hospitality have been far more than we imagined on our journey here. We are keen to begin our discussions with you to preserve peace between our two nations," the prince said with a false smile. He had felt more than uncomfortable from the moment he had spied the first centaur on their journey, and now to be surrounded by those who were possessed of magic, he felt as though a knife was being held to his throat.

"We are honoured by your presence, if you would follow us, we can show you to your rooms and eat before we begin our discussions," Riley smiled kindly and beckoned for the men to follow her.

Berengar had not taken his eyes from her from the moment she had appeared before them and he was the first to step forward after her.

Upon seeing their commander move forward, the soldiers followed, though more timidly with the prince the last to walk through the doors.

Cornelius waited for the prince to enter the castle and fell into step beside him.

"Don't fret, you prince, though there may be

those that bear a grudge against you in these lands, none in this hall would see any harm come to you," Cornelius gave the prince a crooked smile.

"You think there are people here who want to hurt me?" Prince Cynfael sounded shocked at the prospect that individuals rather than a nation would bear him ill-will.

"Of course. The Grand Duchess for one, I know that she has a personal grievance against you, but she was not invited to this event," Cornelius said, stroking his chin.

"Tempest came here?" Prince Cynfael said with shock and horror.

"Yes, about two years ago after you dissolved your engagement. She is a rich and powerful woman, but many were questioning why you would take such an action to break with a woman so beautiful. They feared she was a sorceress or worse, and she was driven from her lands. She came here and found herself not only welcomed but valued. She has a seat on the council to speak for those who live in these lands that do not have magic, and she has been named Grand Duchess of the North. She overseas the governance of all the northern settlements and tribes. She has been a boon to our country, and she is to be wed to a lovely sorcerer from King Latimer's lands. The pair seem to have been made for each other," Cornelius explained.

"Then, if she is so happy, would she wish me ill will?" Prince Cynfael frowned.

"Because you sent assassins to try and kill her on multiple occasions. Women tend to not forget such brutal betrays or breaches of trust - no matter how happy they may be in their new lives," Cornelius replied with a shrug.

Prince Cynfael did not know what to say in reply but meekly nodded his head and walked beside Cornelius without complaint.

Berengar had fallen into step with Riley and the pair walked engaged in polite conversation about the similarity in customs between their two lands and the diversity that existed within the Magistowe boundaries.

On the surface, there did not seem to be much more than a cordial exchange of ideas, but the lounger they talked the more Riley was certain that the man walking beside her was the guardian her parents had spoken of.

For Berengar, he had never felt so drawn to anyone before in his life. There has been sweethearts and women that had thrown themselves into his life, but he had been so focused on his duty and career he had always assumed that a woman and family would come later.

Walking beside a sorceress of such beauty and grace, he found himself bewitched and wanting to find anything to speak of so that his conversation with her would not end.

Prince Cynfael was impressed by the rooms that had been prepared for the guests in the castle, and was more impressed by the hustle and bustle of the practical governance of Magistowe.

Disputes were presided over quickly with three elders chosen to hear the petitions from both sides before weighing the evidence before arriving at a judgement together.

Newcomers and refugees were welcomed and assigned to a region of the country where their talents would be of the most use. Everyone that came to Magistowe was expected to contribute to the country, whether it was through physical labour, the advancement of learning, art, music, poetry, prose, dance, planning, storytelling, or even gardening. Crafts were highly sought after, and good orators to stand and speak the daily news to the masses were often in short supply. It did not matter what age, race, creed, or how intelligent those coming to Magistowe were, there was always something that they could do to add to the fabric of the society.

As magic was the primary source of wealth within the country, there was no shortage of food, water, or shelter. Basic items for the homes were conjured or created, and once people were settled, they were able to change whatever they liked about their dwellings through trade at the markets across the land.

Fine pieces of hand-crafted furniture were sold for the highest prices as they as much art as they were items for function, and even Riley's imagination could not replicate the depth, detail and soul that each of these unique pieces possessed.

There was also gold for trade with other nations and for areas where non-magicals wanted to trade their skills to earn a living.

The elderly were not cast aside either, as they had more to contribute in experience and their knowledge of their cultures and histories were invaluable.

Scribes would visit them to listen and record all that they said, and the scrolls and tombs filled with their words were stored in the great library on the ground floor of the sorcerers' school.

The banquet that was held in the honour of the guests completely eclipsed the feast they had in the small town outside the city. Food kept appearing on the tables for hours until the visitors could eat no more. Then the doors to the hall were opened and as the guests were escorted to the central meeting chamber, the people of the city were invited to finish what remained from the feast so that nothing was wasted.

A round table sat at the heart of the central meeting room and there were chairs enough around the table for the council members present and the retinue of the prince.

Cornelius was formally introduced as the first mage of the council. Mairi, an extremely tall, gaunt and hawkish looking woman was introduced as the second mage. Roweena, a woman who looked to be twice as old as Cornelius, was the third mage. Drusus, a tanned and muscular man with a shock of white hair was the fourth mage. Hellebore, a small person with long purple hair was the fifth mage, and for as long as Berengar tried, he could not decide whether they were male or female. Leander, a man in his forties who was quick to smile and towered over even Mairi, was the sixth mage. Natrix, a dark-skinned man with a silken voice was the final mage of the council.

Meridier, a faun with a sweet disposition was the non-human member of the council who spoke for the magical creatures of the land. Host, a young man with trembling hands and an infatuation with Meridier appeared on behalf of the Grand Duchess Tempest to speak for the non-magical people.

With Riley at their head, the council numbered ten in all, and each had an equal voice to speak with. There was a rational way in which discussions were held. Cornelius, as the first mage, was the chair of the meeting. He invited parties to speak when they indicated they had something to say and as such, tempers were kept in check and each person was able to speak their piece.

For five days the council came to meet with their guests and discussed every possible worry that the kingdoms had and the council spoke at great length as to how the land of Magistowe was governed.

Berengar dreaded the end of the meetings as he knew that each night, Riley would leave the castle and return to her home outside the city, accompanied by Cornelius, Mairi and Drusus.

To begin with he had been quite jealous of the strikingly handsome man, especially when he left the first meeting beside Riley, but Cornelius had been quick to explain that Drusus was a man with no interest in women.

But now that the mission was drawing to a close, Berengar was filled with a sense of panic that he would be parted from Riley forever.

There was no way that he could remain in the country as he had duties to return home to, and there was no situation he could see where Riley could be persuaded to come back with him.

Prince Cynfael brought the negotiations to a close on the sixth day, and Berengar said a long and lingering goodbye to Riley. She had smiled sadly but had shown little regret at their parting.

She knew that if he truly was her guardian then he would return to her and if he was not, then this was simply a fleeting moment in time.

On the journey back to King Ruettigur there were no creatures lining the route they took and their absence was far more unnerving than their presence had been. Prince Cynfael was certain that they were being watched and did not feel safe until they had crossed into his father's lands.

Upon their return, Prince Cynfael and Berengar reported directly to the king and told him of all they had learned, seen and thought of the country of Magistowe.

The king listened silently, his brow furrowed and his eyes dark. When the pair were finished, the king grunted and dismissed them both from his sight. He called his adviser, Arcanthus, to meet with him and discuss what his son and the Knight-Marshal had told him.

For three days they spoke behind a closed door and no one was allowed to enter. At the end of the three days, the king summoned Cynfael and Berengar.

"I believe that you both saw what the sorcerers wanted you to see, that they bewitched your minds the moment you entered their lands. They are hiding their true intentions from us and their magic is a poison, a blight on all lands. We must fight against their evil and wipe it from this world. We shall go to war," the king decreed.

Cynfael and Berengar were both alarmed by the attitude of their king but neither of them could oppose his will and all that they could say in reply was,

"Yes, Your Majesty."

CHAPTER 5

The paranoia of King Ruettigur was not known to the people of Magistowe, but even if they had been told of his desire for war with the magical community, it would have been the least of the council's concerns.

The day after their guests departed from the city, a trader from Ruettigur's kingdom arrived bearing grave tidings of black magic and a dark wizard.

"I am sorry to ask for an audience, I know that you are all busy," the merchant had said apologetically.

"It is no trouble, we appreciate the seriousness of the matter you wish to bring before the council," Riley replied kindly.

"There has been a lot of talk about a dark presence in our land, livestock have been sick and harvests have failed. For the most part, it is all things that seem to be unconnected and that the prejudice against magic was the only reason for the rumours. But there is something else. It is like the life is being stolen from the land itself, and a plague has started to spread amongst the farming communities," the merchant explained nervously.

"I see. That is most concerning indeed. I must speak with those amongst the tribes that are closest to the earth immediately," Meridier said abruptly and excused herself from the meeting.

"Mairi, Natrix and I will use our powers to search for any traces of dark magic," Roweena said firmly.

"We should begin at once, there is no time to lose if a dark wizard is raising a plague," Natrix said in agreement and the three sorcerers departed from the meeting.

"Cornelius, Drusus and I will come with you to Ruettigur's lands. We must speak to the king about this plague before blame for it falls upon us," Riley announced.

"Leander, Hellebore and I will remain her and

oversee the lands. Whatever Meridier, Natrix, Mairi and Roweena discover we shall send word of the moment we can," Tempest said as the council was formerly brought to a close.

It took no time at all for Riley, Cornelius and Drusus to prepare themselves to travel with the merchant.

The journey to Ruettigur's lands was not a short one and by the time the sorcerers had passed into the kingdom, the plague had already begun to spread rapidly throughout the population of not only Ruettigur's kingdom, but Latimer's lands as well as the four other kings.

The king's reception for his guests was cold and unwelcoming, something the sorcerers had expected.

"Do you come here to make your demands before you will lift this blight you have cast over us?" the king demanded of the trio as they entered his throne room.

"It is not of our doing, sire. We came to warn

you that news of the plague had reached us and offer our assistance in bringing an end to this darkness," Riley said calmly but firmly.

"You travel a great distance to lie," the king sneered in reply.

"Sire, it is no lie. We are here to help all of you. Your people have been speaking of dark wizard, and we believe that they are right. Evil magic is at work here but it does not come from Magistowe," Drusus said with a slight edge of contempt in his voice.

"Then find the source of this plague and put an end to it. Then we might believe you," the king snapped.

"We shall do so, sire," Riley replied flatly.

"My Knight-Marshal shall go with you, he will be my eyes and ears and ensure that you do not plot to overthrow when my kingdom is so weakened by your work," the king snapped.

Cornelius did not speak a word whilst they were in the presence of the king, but the moment they were out of the audience chamber, he shook his head.

"There is dark magic at work here and it is already affecting the king's mind," he sighed.

"Yes, there is some ill at work here. We should not linger," Drusus agreed.

"The Knight-Marshal will be waiting for us with our horses. We should not keep him waiting," Riley sighed and could not hide the slight smile that curled at the corner of her mouth.

"We should be wary of Berengar too, at least for the moment. We do not know what effect the darkness has had upon him," Cornelius warned. But the warning fell on deaf ears as Riley giddily made her way to the stables to meet with Berengar again.

Chapter 6

Berengar did not know why he had been ordered to report to the stables, and had a sinking feeling in the pit of his stomach. The king had not been in his right mind since the envoys had returned from their mission, and since the plague had begun to ravage all kingdoms, he feared that he was now on a mission that would bring harm to Magistowe.

He was pleasantly surprised when instead of soldiers or assassins, he was met by Riley, Cornelius and Drusus.

"Well met, Knight-Marshal, we are glad to see you once more. The king sends us on a mission to end this plague, with you to oversee our actions," Cornelius announced in his loudest voice so that all heads on the street turned in their direction.

"Did you hear that? The Knight-Marshal is going to stop the plague," one of the stablehands said as he put down his pitchfork and turned to appeal to the people in the street.

Cheers went up from the people who pressed forward to tell Berengar how he was a hero and how much the people loved him.

Riley and Drusus couldn't help but smile at Cornelius' antics as they prepared their horses for the return journey. By the time they were ready, the crowd had completely forgotten that they were sorcerers and focused only on the departure of Berengar with all their hopes for a cure to the afeared plague.

The three guests rode in a line behind Berengar almost as an honour guard as the heroic figure left his city. People had run to spread the word in every corner of the city, and then to the kingdom beyond, that there was hope and Berengar was the one bringing it to them.

People lined the streets, cheering, throwing flowers in the path of his horse, it was just like the stories that Riley's mother used to tell her of brave knights on dangerous quests for their nations.

The cheers of the people lingered in the air long after they had left the city and travelled into the wilds. Riley did not know where to begin searching for answers to the plague but she knew where to seek the wisdom to help her.

Magistowe City was not build directly on top of the wellspring, but as the city had begun to grow, Riley had been concerned that the city was grow over the top of it without meaning to and it would leave the wellspring vulnerable if it were not properly protected.

When Drusus had arrived in Magistowe, Riley had given the home she had first created to him so that he could live close to Cornelius and learn from the older man.

It gave Riley the perfect excuse to move her own home and she made it so that the house not only blocked the entrance to the wellspring, but gave have secret access to it in order to better protect it.

Her new home was not far from her old home

and it allowed for the other magical members of the council to have their homes built between hers and Cornelius' house.

"Where do we begin on this search for the cause of the plague and a cure?" Berengar asked when they were a decent distance from the city.

"We shall begin with speaking with the other members of the council. Grand Duchess Tempest has been sending out her men in search of more information about the plague since we first had word of it. Our healers are trying to learn all that they can of this plague so they might make a cure. Other members of the council are searching for any sources of dark magic that may be influencing such a plague," Riley explained.

"I see, then you already had some suspicions about the plague? Is that why you came?" Berengar asked with a frown.

"Many merchants and traders travel through Magistowe to curate a varied inventory of exotic goods, they bring with them news, rumours and information. Kings and Knight-Marshals do not use this resource and so are often a little poorer for it," Cornelius replied airily with a dismissive wave of his hand.

"Rumours are a dangerous thing," Berengar warned.

"Unsubstantiated rumours are dangerous, but if one investigates rumours or can point to a truth that contradicts a rumour, they are no more dangerous than a newborn lamb," Drusus replied. "Perhaps if your king was not so ready to believe rumour and wild speculation, he would not have -"

"Enough, Drusus. We do not need to speak of that now. We are far enough away from prying eyes. Cornelius, if you would make the preparations," Riley said abruptly as she reined her horse to a halt and dismounted.

"Very well," Cornelius agreed and dismounted, handing his reins to Riley.

Drusus also dismounted and held his horse

whilst casting dark looks at Berengar. Berengar was entirely confused as to why the party had stopped and only dismount because everybody else had.

Cornelius was busying himself drawing lines with the end of his staff. The staff had been packed across the back of his horse whilst they rode and though Berengar had not thought of it until now, he was not convinced the old man need the staff as a walking stick.

Cornelius took his time drawing the lines in the earth but when he was done he walked to the centre of his work and began to utter something under his breath. A few moments later he slammed the end of his staff into the ground and the markings he had made in the earth began to glow blue.

"It is ready," Cornelius called and Berengar watched as Drusus and Riley lead their horses over the blue marks to where Cornelius stood.

"Hurry and join us, or be left behind," Riley said to Berengar.

The Knight-Marshal looked terrified at the prospect of crossing the blue glowing lines, but he was all too aware of what would happen to him if the king discovered the mages had left him behind.

He took a deep breath and tentatively led his horse over the first of the blue lines. Nothing happened, so he continued forwards until he was almost next to Riley, then there was a blinding flash and he felt like his head was being ripped from his shoulders.

Pain shot through his temples and he passed out.

"It has been a rather interesting day for the lad, poor thing, I am sure he will recover in no time under your care. I will speak with Tempest about kingdom etiquette and dining habits so we can accommodate our guest," Cornelius' voice filtered through the black of Berengar's mind as he struggled to find his way back to consciousness.

"Will you be all right, alone with him?" Drusus

asked in a rather protective way.

"I will be fine. There is no soldier born yet that can harm me, and I doubt this Knight-Marshal is any different. Besides, he is one man in a city of thousands of magic users, he is hardly going to cause problems. You both have far greater concerns that require immediate attention, so please, focus your minds on those. Should I need assistance, I will send up a signal," Riley said calmly and there seemed to be a hint of humour in her voice.

"Very well, until this evening," Cornelius said. Berengar was aware of the sound of footsteps leaving the room he was in, a door opening and closing and then the feeling that he was alone in the room with Riley.

"You can open your eyes, though you may want to shade your eyes," Riley said. Her voice sounded very close to Berengar and he found himself raising his arm to his face to shade his eyes as he opened them.

The light stung and his head felt heavy, as

though it were filled with lead, but as his eyes adjusted to the light in the room and the momentary stinging passed, he realised he was in a bedroom and lying on what he could only assume was Riley's bed.

Riley was stood, looking out of a window as Berengar managed to fight against the feeling he was going to faint again and sat up.

"What happened?" Berengar asked as he held his pounded head in his hands.

"You have been close to the influence of a dark sorcerer. It confirmed what we feared, that this plague is borne of magic, but not any magic found here in Magistowe. Whoever has created this dark curse is likely in your own kingdom. The blue light was a counter curse against the darkness, though your reaction to the removal of its influence was far more violent than expected," Riley sighed.

"Is that why you dismounted? To force me from my horse so I would not fall if I was so affected?" Berengar sighed as he rubbed his temples.

"Partly. But the spell was not just to remove any dark influences from your mind. It was a spell to transport us instantly to the city. Even for those of us who have travelled in such a manner for many years, it is still disorientating and the horses often lose their footing when we land in the courtyard," Riley explained and moved to hand Berengar a cool cloth to press against his forehead.

"When will this pain pass?" Berengar asked as he gratefully accepted the cloth.

"A few minutes to a few hours if you exposure to the darkness was short-lived, months if you were subjected to its influence for lounger. But there is a way that will perhaps help. Are you able to stand?" Riley asked.

"I think so," Berengar said and managed to gingerly push himself off of the bed and stagger forwards. Riley stepped forward and used her own body to steady him.

Berengar felt his heart pounding so hard against

his ribcage that he thought it would burst from his chest at any second. The feeling of Riley's hands on his chest and back, the strength of her body and the gentleness of her touch seemed set to drive him to the edge of madness as he resisted the urge to lean in and kiss her.

"Come, step slowly. We are in no hurry," Riley said kindly and helped him to take a few steps forward. Her fingers could feel his muscled chest under his clothes as she stopped him from toppling forwards. She could feel his heart beating as fast as her own as they slowly inched their way across the room to the bedroom door.

As they passed through the doorway and into the kitchen, Berengar found that his head felt slightly better and was able to walk more easily. Riley steered him across the floor towards a wall that she seemed intent on reaching.

With every step Berengar took towards the wall, he found that his head was returning to normal and that Riley's assistance was no lounger required. When they reached the wall, Riley stepped away from Berengar's side and paused,

"What I am about to show you can never be revealed to another living soul. Should you betray this trust not only shall you die but so shall every soul that you tell. Do you understand?" Riley asked seriously.

Though Berengar recognised the threat in her voice, something told him that such a threat was justified and he readily agreed.

Riley reached out towards the wall and as her fingers touched the wood panel, blue light sprang forth in patterns across the wood and the panel disappeared, leaving a tunnel in its place.

Without waiting for any comment from Berengar, Riley began to walk down the tunnel with purpose and the Knight-Marshal hurried to follow her. The darkness in the tunnel seemed to swallow them both up and they walked in the silent blackness, neither being able to see through it, but it did not last long. As soon as Berengar began to worry that he had taken a wrong path or been turned around, a blue light flickered at the end of the tunnel.

Each step he took brought him closer to the light until he eventually found himself standing beside Riley in a great stone cavern with a large fountain at the centre.

"What is that?" Berengar asked with amazement as he eyed the fountain. It was not water pouring forth from it and cascading to the pool below, but-

"Magic. It is the wellspring of all magic in this world and I am the conduit for the power in this wellspring. Through me it flows out into the world and gives powers to all those it touches or deems worthy," Riley explained.

"You have done well," a voice sounded in the cavern before Berengar could speak and his eyes widened with fear.

"Thank you, father," Riley replied and out of the pool of magic the figure of an old knight appeared.

There was something familiar in the face of the knight that Berengar could not place.

"This is your father?" Berengar asked with surprise.

"Not really. The conduit allows me to reach out to those I love in the world beyond and bring forth their wisdom and the wisdom of the wellspring in their voices. They cannot linger long and it is only by my power that they can now appear," Riley replied.

"Then you summoned him?" Berengar frowned.

"No, but there will be a reason the wellspring has brought him forth," Riley explained.

"There is a very good reason," Godfrey replied. "I see that you have found your guardian."

"Guardian?" Berengar asked, feeling the headache rapidly returning.

"Every conduit is at threat from the darkness and as such a guardian for that conduit is born to protect her. You, sir, are that guardian," Godfrey said firmly to Berengar.

"I am sworn to the service of another already. I cannot be a guardian," Berengar argued with the figure.

"I was sworn to the service of King Latimer's father. I was his Knight-Marshal and when I met Adele I knew that I had to forsake everything for her. I think you already know in your heart that my daughter is the person that you should be with and pledged to rather than an ungrateful king," Godfrey said kindly but Berengar suddenly knew when he recognised the figure.

"Sir Godfrey Aldereck? You trained me as a young squire as none in my own land would take me. When you left, I was sent home and had to be taken on by another knight. You abandoned me for a woman?" Berengar demanded.

"You were not abandoned. Sir Estned training you upon your return home was not a happy accident. I chose him and asked him to take you on as his squire. I made sure that you would still be able to rise to the rank you craved. You lost nothing in my departure," Godfrey replied and Berengar could not find a way to reply.

"Though I am glad that you have confirmed what I long suspected, it is not the matter of my guardian that brings us here," Riley said, trying to divert the conversation from an uncomfortable course.

"You wish advice on how to find the darkness?" the figure asked with a bemused expression on his face.

"I do," Riley said eagerly.

"I cannot tell you anything you do not already know about its location. But I will tell you of what is to come. Not just the immediate future, but the fate of all the lands. The forces of darkness shall always seek out this wellspring, seek to corrupt it and the light must push back. There can be no evil without light and no light without evil. The two forces exist in a delicate balance that must be maintained. Should one or other gain too much and snuff the other out, the world will descend into darkness and chaos," he father explained and Riley nodded her understanding.

"What can I do to stop the darkness from gain too much power?" Riley asked.

"Protect the city and you protect the wellspring," her father replied. "Rest, both of you, in this place. Let the magic heal your minds and souls. When you wake in the morning, you shall know what must be done."

CHAPTER 7

Riley sent word to the council that she would not be able to meet with them that evening and told only Cornelius that she was communing with the wellspring. He was the only other person in all of Magistowe that was appear of the presence of the source of all magic, though he was not entirely sure where it could be found.

Berengar slumped to the ground with his back against a cave wall and watched the magic cascading down the fountain.

"Do you truly believe that I am fated to be your guardian?" Berengar asked her after the silence between them had stretched to an hour.

"I do. I have known it since the first time my eyes fell upon you when you arrived with Prince Cynfael. My heart beats in time with yours and slightest touch from you seems to awaken music in my soul," Riley replied with a shrug.

"That is simple attraction. It is not the call of fate demanding that I give up all that I have vowed to protect for one soul," Berengar replied.

"If that is so, lie with me tonight. Let our attraction give way to whatever passion stirs in our bodies, and, if in the morning, you still believe that this is nothing more than attraction, I will not bind you to any service nor make a single demand of you," Riley said seriously.

Berengar looked up sharply at her to see if she was serious, and when he saw that she was, he smiled and held out his hand to her.

Riley moved across the floor to take his hand and allowed him to pull her into his arms. He held her firmly and gently stroked her cheek, moving her hair from her eyes and when he could no lounger resist her, he kissed her.

Berengar had never known such passion or connection with another being before in his life. From the feeling of her body pressed against his to the simple pleasure of lying beside her as she slept, he understood that it was not simple attraction that pulled the pair together.

He barely slept as his mind reeled at what he must do and tried to fathom how he could leave the service of the king without harming the woman he had to protect.

Riley slept peacefully and well, and was gratified when Berengar awakened her gently with a kiss.

"I pledged all I am to you and your protection," Berengar whispered to her.

"What will you tell Ruettigur?" Riley asked as she ran her fingers through his hair.

"I do not know. I spent the night worrying about it, but I could not find an answer. Perhaps it is something I shall not have to do. The plague may claim the king and Prince Cynfael would be much more inclined to allow me to leave his service," Berengar replied.

"Well then, whilst we wait for such a terrible fate for another life, there is much to do here. The wellspring has healed the damage the darkness did to your mind and soul, and I am almost certain you cannot be harmed by the plague now. But there is more that must be done to protect this city and the people in all the settlements of this land," Riley explained.

"Once your lands are safe, then you will act against the darkness?" Berengar asked.

"Yes, though we shall need to learn more before we can hold him in check and stop the plague. But we shall move as quickly as possible," Riley assured him.

The council were waiting for the pair that morning when they arrived at the sorcerers' tower. Cornelius had made sure that everyone would be present and hurried them along. There was a great deal that the old man seemed to know that he chose not to share with the other council members, and there were times when it almost seemed some of those secrets might slip out.

Now was one of those times. He seemed to be agitated and overly excited for reasons no-one else could understand. Drusus had woken in the small hours of the morning to find candles lit in Cornelius' windows and a great deal of noise coming from his home. Drusus had not pried into the affair with Cornelius but he had mentioned it to Leander when he had awoken that morning.

Grand Duchess Tempest was thrilled to see the Knight-Marshal and welcomed him warmly to the council chamber, bidding him sit beside her. Berengar had tried to politely declined, but Riley was keen to have at least a little fun with him and insisted he sit with the Grand Duchess.

Meridier, Natrix, Mairi and Roweena were all sat together with grave looks on their faces. Leander sat with Drusus and Hellebore and the three seemed to all be avoiding looking directly at Cornelius.

Riley's chair sat upon a plinth that was raised

above the other chairs of the council around the round table. When visiting dignitaries came, it was removed from the hall to promote the sharing of ideas as equal voices, but in private conference, Cornelius had insisted that Riley's chair was set higher so that all in the room would remember that she was not only the founder but leader of their country and deserved every respect that should be afforded to her.

"There is grave news that we all must share. From the looks on each of your faces, each piece of the puzzle may be more dire than the last. But for now, we must set aside our immediate concerns over the darkness and this plague and fix our eyes on the future," Riley said gravely.

"The future? How can there be a future if we do not act now to stop this plague and the threat of evil?" Meridier demanded, her voice almost shrill with anger.

"There will be a future if we act now to preserve it and not simply react to an obvious danger," Riley replied calmly.

"And what is it that you propose?" Roweena asked with a tilt of her head.

"We set wards and magical protections in the very foundations of the earth, weave them into our streets and buildings and even the hearts of our people. These wards and seals will act not only as barriers to the darkness in the future, but will protect our nation from the plague and the hand of the darkness," Riley replied confidently.

"Are there not already such protections in place?" Leander asked with a frown.

"To an extent," Cornelius replied. "Not on the scale that Riley is suggesting though. There are barriers to protect against direct curses and weaker forms of dark magic. These wards, seals and barriers our leader suggests are far stronger and would ensure that even after all civilisations have fallen to dust and nature has reclaimed the lands, the magical enchantments will remain."

"Is that the full extent of your plan?" Tempest

asked with interest.

"No, all magic that involves necromancy, curses, manipulating life forces, sacrifices, in fact anything linked to dark magic is to be outlawed. It shall be punishable by cutting off any practitioners who ignore this abolishment from magic itself," Riley said seriously.

A tense silence fell over the chamber. Berengar was not sure why such a statement should warrant such a reaction and he did not want to ask given how seriously the council took the suggestion.

"This may not prove to be popular," Natrix said slowly. "I do not disagree with this course of action, but there are a great many who came here because of the freedom to practise their craft. Imposing laws now upon what is and isn't acceptable will be difficult."

"Difficult it shall be, but I believe that Riley is correct and that it is necessary. The other nations fear our community because of those dark arts and the misunderstanding that all of us dabble in such things.

When this plague is brought to an end, it would be foolish to think there would be no repercussion for those who live here," Mairi said firmly.

"She is correct. King Ruettigur is already keen to declare war on your people without the excuse of the plague giving fuel to propaganda against you," Berengar said sadly.

"Then we have no choice. Those who do not wish to be bound by this law must leave the lands of Magistowe. They shall have three days to depart if they do not wish to comply. I shall have the criers informed at once so word can be spread," Hellebore said as they stood and strode across the chamber and disappeared through the giant doors.

The criers were each informed and immediately scattered to all corners of the country to spread word of the council's decision and the reasoning for it.

The non-magical humans heard the news and found some comfort in the decision and the reasoning for it, but the question of restricting freedoms was raised and discussed over many rounds of drinks for weeks after.

The magical creatures found no issue with such a decree as none of their magics was based in such dark arts and the creatures that were considered dark hunters and curses had not migrated to the Magistowe lands, preferring to prey on humans that could not raise magical defences against them.

But amongst the sorcerers there were bitter and almost violent disputes that broke out almost as soon as the criers began to spread the word.

Some who had never thought of practising such magic decided to leave Magistowe for fear of other restrictions, and freedoms they might be denied.

By the end of the third day, four hundred sorcerers had left the country and their departure had sadden many, but there was nothing that could be done to convince them to stay.

Riley had given almost no thought to those who had chosen to leave, they would be at risk of the influence of the darkness, as well as other dangers, but their departure was their own choice.

Instead she had focused her mind on what had to be accomplished to protect those that remained. Scrolls of ancient protection spells, the strongest seals and wards were all brought from the library and two thousand sorcerers that were skilled in such magic were summoned to perform the incantations.

Riley had her own magic to weave and she knew that it must be done from the privacy of the wellspring. Whilst her people placed the strongest magic they knew around every corner of the land, Riley knelt before the wellspring with only Berengar by her side.

She did not speak a word but her thoughts sprang to life all about them. Magic that would seek out and battle dark forces in the form of wolves, bears, and griffins was woven before the Knight-Marshal's eyes and he was astounded at Riley's capabilities. He watched as she infused the earth with magical traps and walls that could be activated with a simple flick of her wrist.

For the weeks that it took the enchanters to weave the magic from the scrolls across the land of Magistowe, Riley used the wellspring to place even more intricate magical defences.

The school seemed to lie at the heart of the defences and a chamber was even created deep underneath it that the magic seemed to be focused around.

When they were finished Riley was certain her people were safe and the council was reconvened to share all they had learned about the darkness.

Chapter 8

From all the evidence gathered by the council, it was clear that the darkness and source of the plague could be found in Ruettigur's kingdom.

Riley was firm in her decision that of all the council members, only she should set out to face and battle with the evil force with Berengar at her side. She was adamant that the others remain behind to protect and maintain life in Magistowe and make preparations for any retaliatory action the other kingdoms might bring against them.

Natrix and Drusus were not comfortable with Riley going alone and suggested that she take at least some of the more promising young sorcerers along to help her in her crusade.

Ry, Jynx, Jeren, and Sen were the most promising sorcerers of their generation and were all most eager to be chosen to accompany Riley on her journey to stop the plague. For them it was as much a journey of discovery and a chance to learn as it was a dangerous assignment with their leader.

Berengar sent word to King Ruettigur that the source of the plague had been found in his lands and that they now rode to confront it. The king sent a patrol to the border to accompany the sorcerers and assist them in their task.

The soldiers outnumbered the mages three to one, but it was the soldiers who were jumpy and on their guard. The tension between the two groups was unbearable and the lounger they travelled together, the more distrusted festered.

Riley and Berengar knew they could not spend their nights in each others arms whilst they journeyed with the group, but subtle kindness he showed towards Riley and the small gestures of affection did not go unnoticed.

It was on the fifth day of their journey that the trouble truly began. Berengar brought Riley the breakfast he had cooked for her and as he handed her the pewter plate, one of his soldiers knocked the plate from her hand, causing the food to cascade to the ground.

"What do you think you are doing?" Berengar demanded as he angrily glared at the soldier.

"The witch has clearly taken your mind. You are bewitched, sir, and we can no lounger stand idly by as she turns you into a thrall of her dark spells," the soldier replied and drew his sword with a flourish.

Riley did not move or seem to feel at all threatened by the act.

The four young sorcerers, on the other hand, took great exception to the accusation and without waiting for any word or action from their leader, they attacked the soldiers.

Berengar was not exempt from their onslaught of magic, but not a single spell could harm him. Riley had enchanted his armour to protect him from all magic when she had created the defences of

Magistowe and the lack of damage the young sorcerers did to him seem to enrage them further.

Though their spells were effective, the soldiers were not easily defeated. The fighting between the two groups was fierce and not even the shouts of Riley and Berengar, or their attempts to intervene could bring a stop to it.

As the fighting worsened, Riley realised that the hand of the darkness was fuelling their mutual hatred. There was was no word that could be said to break the hold that the dark powers had over them now and if Riley and Berengar did not want to shed needless blood, their only chance was to flee and hope that both sides would come to their senses.

Neither the soldiers nor the young mages seemed to notice the abrupt departure of their leaders, so focused were they on the destruction of their perceived enemy.

Riley and Berengar made for the closest village as fast as they could. There was no doubt in Berengar's mind that all sixteen members of their company would die at that camp and he bitterly regretted being unable to rescue them from their hatred.

"What do we do now?" Berengar asked with a heavy sigh, as the pair sat in the tavern and awaited a breakfast of whatever hot meal was on offer that morning.

"We should hide ourselves, and travel as quietly, and unnoticed as we can. I can cast a spell to change the appearance of our clothing so that we do not need to search for anything to hide. We listen to rumours and speak to whatever merchants we can to discover where the darkness is hiding and who the source of the plagues is," Riley said in a hushed voice.

Berengar readily agreed to her plan and after she had cast the enchantment, Berengar's armour had transformed into the worn clothes of a farmer, and Riley's robes now looked like the clothes of a travelling merchant.

They began their search in the village as they

purchased supplies for their long journey to the next village. There were risks to using magic whilst in the kingdom of King Ruettigur and with the hysteria of the plague and the ill-feeling towards Magistowe that festered in the country, so Berengar and Riley had agreed that it would be best if they purchased and travelled as though they were simple common folk.

Riley made sure to create a small amount of items that they could use to convince people they were a travelling merchant and her new guard and used her magic to make their horses appear as though they were dishevelled ponies.

It was a small ruse but enough to divert attention away from the pair.

They stayed at the inn for one night and departed the following morning. They journeyed from town to town, trading information and goods as they went until Berengar was almost convinced that this would be what they spent the rest of their lives doing.

Six months passed in the blink of an eye. There

were adventures to be had on the roads between towns and a great deal happened that strengthened the bond between the pair. But the darkness did not find them, nor did they fall victim to the plague.

But everywhere they went there was talk of the plague, of a man called Arcanthus and the deteriorating mind of the king. The most alarming rumour was the disappearance of Prince Cynfael, his intended and their retinue.

"Who is this Arcanthus? Do you know him?" Riley had asked after his name had been mentioned in three of the villages they passed through.

"He was a man of no real importance. His father was a lesser noble and had pressured the king into accepting Arcanthus into his court as one of the many advisers he has. The king has men from all over the kingdom to lend their voices to decisions," Berengar explained. "In reality most of the voices are ignored and the Duke of Erenthorpe and the Duke of Wakewater are the only two voices that carry any weight. When I left, Arcanthus was the lowest of those at court, even the squires could order him about. But now, he seems to have more power than the two dukes combined," Berengar said with a shake of his head.

"Then this man has amassed great power and influence in a matter of months," Riley sighed.

"You think that he is the source of this darkness?" Berengar frowned.

"I do. At least he bears investigating. Those who have such meteoric rises are often not all they appear to be," Riley replied.

"What should we do then? Go straight to the capital?" Berengar asked.

"No, not directly. We need somewhere quiet and private first where I can use my abilities to try and learn all that I can about this Acanthus," Riley said with a slight shake of her head.

"Then we shall go to my estate. We can remain undisturbed there," Berengar gave her a wry half-smile.

"Very well," Riley allowed with amusement. "How far is it from here?"

"About a three day ride. We should go as soon as possible so that we can be in the next village before nightfall," Berengar replied. "The roads around these parts are not safe to travel outside of settlements after nightfall."

Chapter 9

Berengar's estate was a welcome sight after their time travelling as merchants. His servants had begun to worry due to his long absence and were relieved to see their master was healthy, whole, and home again.

Riley was introduced to the steward of the estate and the housekeeper, and was met with the suspicion and dark looks she had come to expect when Berengar mentioned that she was a sorceress.

But neither made any remarks, instead greeting her with forced and strained civility.

Berengar informed the housekeeper a private room was required for his guest and that she was not to be disturbed for any reason.

Riley was shown through the large house, up the steep steps of one of the back towers and to a rather cold room at the top of it.

"Will this suffice?" the housekeeper asked in a

tone that was frostier than the room temperature.

"Yes, thank you," Riley said warmly and did not react at all when the housekeeper huffed from the room and slammed the door behind her.

When Riley was certain the housekeeper had gone, she closed her eyes and took a deep breath. She imagined the room as she wanted it to be. The chairs, cushions, throws, window coverings, and rugs. The tables, books, bed, and blankets. Every tiny detail she agonised over until she had built the picture in her mind.

When she was satisfied with how the room looked, she breathed deep and opened her eyes. As she breathed out the room around her began to take shape according to her vision.

Magic swirled about the tower, added a mezzanine floor with a wooden ladder up to it. Her bed lay on the mezzanine floor along with a chamber pot, basin and jug filled with cool, clean water.

A fireplace came into being in place of one of

the windows and the temperature of the room improved immediately. The other windows were covered with leaded glass to keep out the cold, though they were all lathed so they could be opened if the weather changed.

A chaise lounge and two armchairs covered with cushions sat around a low table, and there were other tables and chair sets spread around the room.

"Good enough," Riley said to herself with mild satisfaction. There was a great deal of work she had to do, but at least now she was comfortable.

Before she began her work, she used the basin to wash herself and feel rejuvenated. She expected that the housekeeper would come at some point to summon her for dinner, but she reflected on Berengar's words and realised that she would have to provide her own food until she was finished working.

She had summoned a large, metal bowl and placed it on one of the tables. Using some of the vellum and a quill she had crafted, she wrote down everything she knew about Acanthus from the rumours they had heard on their travels.

Once she was sure she had written ever last scrap of information down, she tore up the vellum and dropped the pieces in the pot.

Using a long taper, lit from the fireplace, she set fire to the vellum and watched a purple flame spring up from the burning pieces.

Riley stared into the flames and waited for something to happen. She had used this method for diving before, but she was not prepared for what she was about to see.

One moment the flames were glowing purple, the next they were black, the torches, lanterns and the fire in the grate had also turned black.

A dark voice called out to her from the flames and tried to draw her to them. She felt pure dread in the pit of her stomach and the trauma of her parents death was something she began to relieve again and again.

"Enough!" she cried as she managed to still her mind and her own magic flashed around the room, extinguishing all the fires.

Sweat poured from her forehead and she was panting heavily. There was no doubt in her mind as to who Acanthus was, but what she didn't know was when she should face him.

As she knelt on the floor, there were pounding feet on the stairs and the door to her room was flung open by Berengar.

"What happened?" he asked, with eyes wide with fear.

"Acanthus is the darkness, or at least it has a hold on him. I cannot be certain which," Riley said with a shake of her head. "Why do you ask? What happened outside of this room?"

Berengar moved slowly across the room and took Riley by the hand, guiding her to the chaise lounge.

"All the fires, lights, torches and braziers turned

to black fire and a great feeling of dread and fear was felt by all. This darkness must be dealt with before its power grows any further," Berengar said firmly.

"Indeed. For Acanthus to wield so much power will, no doubt, be poisoning the king's mind as well as those close to the throne. It will be dangerous, but we must go now I fear. The longer we wait, the more dire the situation shall become," Riley replied with a sigh.

Berengar kissed her forehead and gently placed his hands over hers.

"Rest for tonight. Sleep in this wondrous room you have created and tomorrow we shall depart. He will not doubt know that we are coming, so we must adequately prepare," Berengar replied.

Riley nodded her head in agreement and lay down to sleep on the chaise lounge. When she opened her eyes again, the light had bled from the sky and night had enveloped the castle.

There was a light tapping at her door as she roused herself from sleep, and she slowly moved to open it. The housekeeper was stood outside the door, looking terrified.

"Dinner, milady," she managed to squeak and beckoned for Riley to follow her. It was obvious to the sorceress that the hand of darkness falling on the Wolf Estate had seemed to have had a rather cowing effect on the staff, whether it was fear of the darkness or fear of her, Riley didn't know but there was a rather sombre mood now entrenched over the castle.

As a result dinner was a quiet affair, but Berengar's cooks had prepared a fine table and Riley felt better for eating. Her mind was focused on the task ahead and so she did not speak much. Berengar was trying to keep his mind from dwelling on what was to come and so he talked at great length and almost needed no response.

When the meal was over, Riley retreated to her tower and was asleep almost as soon as her head touched the pillow.

Berengar did not retire to bed, instead he went

to his study and went through reams of papers. He wrote instructions to those who ran his estate, letters to his family, letters to Magistowe and instructions to the soldiers that served beneath him, all of which were entrusted to his steward to be sent only in the event of his death. When he did get to bed, the sun was already rising.

Riley did not awaken until it was almost noon, and Berengar did not stir for another hour after that. The servants all tried to convince their master to delay for one more day, to rest and go the following morning, but neither the sorceress nor the knight-marshal could be swayed from their mission.

The housekeeper packed some small supplies into saddlebags for the pair and by mid-afternoon the two had set out for the capital.

The two rode in silence and pushed their horses hard. By the time they reached the city, night had fallen and the streets were all but deserted. Fears of the plague had meant that the inns in the city had all been closed as well as all the taverns and playhouse. The brothels were closed to all but the very richest patrons and the markets were visited only for necessities, not luxuries as they had once been.

"Where does Acanthus live?" Riley asked as they drew closer to the palace.

"He has a house to the west, I expect he is waiting for us there," Berengar said gravely.

"Very well, lead on," Riley replied, mirroring his tone.

Soldiers saluted as the knight-marshal passed. They pair had abandoned their disguises on the journey to Berengar's estate and had decided it would be for the best for them to arrive in the city as themselves.

They left their horses at the stable where the military horses were housed and the stable boys promised the knight-marshal to take the very best care of both mounts. Striking out on foot, Berengar led the way down a maze of streets and back alleys to arrive at the area where the richest men in the city all lived.

The gate to Acanthus house had been left open and where a guard would normally have stood, there was none.

Riley drew in her breath as she pushed the gate wide and stepped into the courtyard. The feeling of dread she had in her stomach at encountering this man was making her feel sick, but she did her best to push the feeling aside.

The courtyard was completely empty, which made the hairs on the back of Berengar's neck stand on end. Silence before a battle was always a bad sign as far as he was concerned, and the servant of the darkness knowing they were coming only compounded his anxiety.

The door to the house was ajar and a single light could be seen within.

"Please, be careful," Berengar whispered to Riley as she placed her hand on the door and pushed it wide.

In the centre of the foyer was a candle on a table. Beside the table was a small man dressed in a black cloak with his hair perfectly swept back from his face.

"Knight-Marshal, you have returned to us. We must celebrate," Acanthus said, his words void of all emotion.

"Do you wish to continue this pretence?" Berengar asked impatiently.

"No witty repartee? No discussion of world views? No battle between intelligent minds before the contest of the physical? No, of course not. You were not blessed with weapons for such a clash. But you, girl, you I imagined would wish to ask at least some questions," Acanthus replied, turning all his attention to Riley.

The door behind her slammed shut and all of the shutters on the windows snapped shut in the same instance.

"I only have one question. Why?" Riley asked as

she firmly stood her ground and tried not to fall victim to the fear that was bubbling up inside her.

"Why? A broad and vague question; do better," Acanthus replied.

"Why serve the darkness? Why spread this plague?" Riley clarified.

"Ah, very poor questions. The answer is obvious, power," Acanthus snorted.

"And what would you consider an intelligent question?" Berengar growled.

"How long have you served the darkness? Are you a servant of the darkness or the darkness itself? Are you the one who killed my parents? The list goes on but why waste my time telling these things to those who'll soon be dead," Acanthus shrugged.

"Will you answer those questions?" Riley asked. Acanthus' lips twisted into a cruel and satisfied smile.

"No. I shall answer one and one only. Then I shall rid the world of you before I move on to destroying your precious magical country," Acanthus replied.

"Did you kill my parents?" Riley asked without hesitation. Berengar was slightly taken aback by the speed and seeming lack of thought in the response.

"Yes," Acanthus said. The moment the word dripped off his lips a wave of malice knocked both Riley and Berengar to the ground. The single candle in the room turned black and Acanthus laughed as he seemed be gathering power to him.

Riley lay upon the ground stunned that this man had killed her parents. She had not know how she would react to finding their murderer, but now she had she was filled with fear, dread and hate.

Get up! The voice of her father yelled at her from somewhere deep inside her soul. *Fight!*

Riley staggered to her feet and tried to focus her mind so that she could battle against Acanthus, but Acanthus was too fast. He threw wave after wave of dark, draining magic at her, breaking her concentration every time. She had no defences she could use against his attacks and was so overwhelmed by his onslaught that she could not use her own magic against him.

Her head swam and she felt her strength failing in her arms and legs. Acanthus advanced on her, pushing her back towards a corner that she would be unable to escape from.

She could feel the grip of the darkness closing in on her. It drowned out everything around her, the voice of her father, all thought of Berengar, where she was, what she had to do, Magistowe, had fled from her mind.

There was nothing she could do, and for the second time in her life she felt alone, helpless and terrified.

Acanthus stood over here and looked down upon her with contempt.

"So this is the great hope that those fools died to protect. What a waste," he chuckled to himself and raised his hand to summon the darkness from deep inside his being, but before he could Berengar swung his sword and slammed the hilt into the back of Acanthus' head.

The vessel crumpled to the floor and the intense feels of helplessness and dread fled from the atmosphere. Riley gasped for air as she crawled from the corner and was hauled to her feet by the knight-marshal.

He did not say anything but moved her towards the front door as quickly as possible. With Acanthus unconscious, the seal on the door had released and Berengar did not want to waste the opportunity that he had created.

He threw open the door and half-dragged, half-carried Riley out of the house and hurried back to the barracks as fast as he could persuade her to move.

Riley was in no condition to ride, so the knight-marshal had the stable boys hitch their two horses to one of the carts that normally carried weapons. Instead of ferrying armaments, Berengar loaded Riley into the back of the wagon to rest and hauled himself into the driver's seat.

He did not know what would happen to the city or even his country now that Acanthus knew he had been compromised, but he knew that his reputation and standing in the kingdom would be destroyed. He also knew that anyone seen or known to have helped him would be arrested, if not killed.

He had explained as much to the two stable boys before they had helped with the wagon, and knowing what they faced, they climbed into the back of the wagon with Riley. They had no families to leave behind, no reason to stay in the city.

Less than a half hour had passed since they had left Acanthus' house when the wagon rolled out of the barracks and headed for the eastern gate. Berengar held his breath with every passing second, knowing an alarm would soon be raised. He did not want to fight his way out of the city, but he was prepared to do it if he had to.

The alarm bells began to sound across the city and the orders were passed to close the gates just as the knight-marshal's wagon rolled out of the city. Every fibre of his being told him that they had to move quickly but there was only so fast that horses pulling a wagon with four people in it could go.

They were less than a mile from the city when the gates were opened and a patrol came filing through to chase down the fleeing party. The two stable boys screamed in fear and tried to make themselves as small as possible in the base of the wagon.

Berengar flicked the reins to coax every ounce of speed out of the horses that he could without upsetting the wagon. His heart pounded in his ears and he mentally prepared himself for the battle he knew he had to fight.

Riley had been lying in the wagon, but she now lifted her head and pushed herself to sit up. She looked at the approaching soldiers and in an almost trance like state she said,

"Home."

Berengar blinked. One moment they were fleeing across King Ruettigur's land, the next they were careening down one of the cobble streets of Magistowe.

"Whoa there," Berengar said as he slowly the horses to a walk and marvelled at the magic that had been used to bring them here.

CHAPTER 10

"Who goes there?" a voice called out from the darkness and a lantern appeared from the shadows of a building with an haggard old face peering out from under it.

"Berengar Wolf, Guardian of Riley Sonen. I have Riley with me as well as my two squires," Berengar replied firmly but did not move from the driver's seat.

"Riley?" the old man asked and held the lantern high. It began to rise above his head and shone brighter until the whole street was illuminated. The light revealed a ring of sorcerers all stood around the horses and wagon all looking suspiciously at Berengar. "Call Cornelius!"

"Stay where you are and do not move or we will be forced to kill you," one of the sorcerers called out but Berengar could not tell which one of them had spoken. He stayed still and did not move. The two stable boys took their lead from him and sat quietly in the wagon, making sure that Riley was comfortable and did not move abruptly and upset the horses or the mages that surrounded them.

Berengar expected the wait to be a long one as he knew that Cornelius lived quite far from the district they had appeared in, but he had forgotten that he was not in a city of normal people who had to walk or ride to every destination.

It took mere minutes for Cornelius, Drusus, and Rowena to materialise in front of Berengar on the street. The three looked pale, their faces were drawn, and Cornelius looked much older than he had done just six months before.

"Berengar! Where is she?" Cornelius asked. The old council member recognising the hard looking stranger caused the mages that were gathered to relax.

"In the wagon with the two boys. The darkness - I will tell you when she is with the healers," Berengar said firmly. He knew that discussing such things in the open might cause panic.

"Healers!" Drusus shouted as Rowena and Cornelius rushed to the wagon to see Riley lying in the back of it looking very weak and pained.

"Dear girl!" Rowena gasped. "Boys, help me get her down."

She was a kind woman and despite her own shock and worry for Riley, she could see how scared the two boys in the wagon were. They eagerly jumped to help the sorceress, and very gently lifted Riley out of the wagon and placed her in Rowena's waiting arms.

Four healers has materialised in the road and upon seeing Riley in Rowena's arms rushed over.

"Take her home. She will recover most quickly there," Berengar said and Cornelius nodded his agreement.

"Come Berengar, we must talk and these two boys need some care," Cornelius said and Berengar climbed down from the cart. The two boys jumped down and rushed to the former knight-marshal's side. Two of the mages stepped forward to take charge of the horses and the wagon whilst the rest melted back into the darkness.

The lantern that had been illuminating the street slowly came back down to the waiting hand of the old man, and he too faded back into the shadows.

"Things have become grave I see," Berengar said in a low voice as he fell into step beside Cornelius.

"Indeed they have, but we must speak of such things in the council hall. Once we have spoken you may go to her. She will be safe enough in her own home. What of these two boys?" Cornelius asked.

"They helped us to escape from the darkness but the king, he would have put them to death if they had remained. I suspect that the Grand Duchess might be in need of two hard, working boys," Berengar replied.

"She may well indeed. I have already sent for her and Meridier to come from their homes to join the council. With Riley's return we must meet and talk about everything we have seen, heard and experienced in the last few months. But first, we must speak," Cornelius replied gravely. The normal spark was missing from the man and his good humour had been eroded away to almost nothing.

Drusus walked with the two boys, the giant man picking up the tired boys when they began to falter. The group made their way to the council tower and Drusus took the two boys to find warm beds and good food whilst Cornelius and Berengar continued to the top of the tower.

Cornelius took Berengar to a small room, it was one that the guardian had never seen before and it was not a comfortable room to be in. The walls were stone and there was a great circle carved in the floor that was big enough for just one man to stand in.

"I am sorry for this, but we must be sure. Please stand in the circle," Cornelius instructed. Berengar felt an instant urge to refuse but his better judgement told him that he could trust Cornelius.

Berengar stepped into the circle and the moment he did he felt an intense field of magic bubble up around him.

"May I ask what this is?" Berengar enquired calmly.

"The circle of truth. It allows only for truth to be spoken. If a lie is detected, whether intentional or not, it inflicts pain on the one within it. I am sorry that I must put you through the ordeal of such, but we must know the truth," Cornelius sighed.

"If this is what must be," Berengar shrugged and waited patiently for what was to come.

"What have you been doing for the last six months?" Cornelius asked.

"Travelling with Riley. We posed as a merchant and her guard. We searched for information on the darkness and what was happening in King Ruettigur's kingdom," Berengar replied. The magic did not react to his words.

"No one recognised you?" Cornelius asked.

"Riley used her magic to disguise us," Berengar said. The magic did not react again.

"I see, and what is it that you discovered?" Cornelius asked.

"The darkness hides in the form of a man called Acanthus. He was a very minor figure in the court of King Berengar but in the last six months he has risen in power and prominence," Berengar replied.

"And what did you do with that information?" Cornelius asked.

"We went to confront him, but he overwhelmed Riley. I managed to use the human frailty of his form against him to allow us our escape, but I doubt he will be harmed so easily a second time," Berengar replied.

"I see. And what do you know of the wellspring?" Cornelius asked.

"Riley showed it to me. Her father was within it. He told me I was her guardian," Berengar said finally.

"You may leave the circle," Cornelius said and

Berengar stepped out of it. "Thank you, I am sorry such lengths were necessary."

"Will you do me the courtesy of standing there for my questions?" Berengar asked. A smile flashed across Cornelius' face.

"Of course," the old man said and stepped into the circle.

"I have one question that I need the answer to that I need the circle to ensure truth," Berengar began. "Is there a traitor in your midst?"

Cornelius looked grave and closed his eyes.

"There is, but I do not know who."

"Very well. Is it you?" Berengar asked.

"No," Cornelius said and the magic did not react.

"Then can we adjourn to a more comfortable room to talk instead of this depressing cell?" Berengar asked.

"Why of course, come we shall take to the sitting room," Cornelius said. "Though first I do need your permission to leave the circle."

"You have it," Berengar chuckled and then followed Cornelius out of the room. They went down a few levels before Cornelius open a door to a bright little room. It was filled with books, scrolls, a fire, and a lot of comfortable chairs.

There were a number of small tables that were cleared and close to the chairs for resting books and drinks upon.

When the door was closed, the two men were seated comfortably and tea had been conjured, they began to talk.

"I suppose our fears of a traitor were exposed by my use of the circle?" Cornelius asked as he stirred far too much sugar into his tea.

"Yes, well at least one of the things. The city feels full of paranoia. The mage inquisition when we arrived, your change in demeanour, there are a lot of tells for those who are paying attention," Berengar shrugged.

The door to the room opened and closed as Drusus joined them.

"It has been a difficult few months. There is much that we will speak of when Riley is well enough and the council is assembled, but I will say, her returning to us will bring some hope, though it may be short-lived. She did have some amazing insight to make all those preparations for protecting these lands. We might not be here now if it weren't for all the work she did," Cornelius sighed.

"That is true. Our lands have stayed free of the plague, but war is stirring. Not against us, for the moment, but between the other kingdoms. Those that did not want to stay under the rules Riley imposed have fallen to the influence of the darkness and now serve as agents of chaos abroad," Drusus explained as he sat down.

"Troubling times indeed," Berengar sighed and shook his head.

"Where are the mages that went with you? They

did not return to us," Cornelius asked.

"Dead, or turned. Though I am certain you are both already aware of how ardently I love Riley, and how she loves me in return, it was not something those young sorcerers or my own men found acceptable. They fought over nothing and died for it. I do not doubt that the darkness had influenced their minds, but it was sad none-the-less," Berengar replied.

"Not even a blind man who has spent any length of time in your company could miss your affection for each other," Cornelius laughed.

"I suppose the idealistic are most at risk from the influence of the darkness beyond our borders," Drusus sighed.

"For now, it would be best if none ventured beyond them," Berengar said seriously.

"Sadly it is not that any wish to venture beyond them, but all those that are clamouring to try and live within them. So many have tried to flee the plague and come to our fair country, so many trying to escape war, but we cannot take everyone that simply wishes to leave. Our lands were created for those escaping persecution, those who could not live in peace because of the attitudes towards magic users and creatures. Many of those now trying to come here are the very people that we have escaped. Their attitudes have no changed and allowing them to come here and live puts our own people at risk from their prejudices," Cornelius shook his head.

"Yet, we cannot turn away those in need. It is a situation that we cannot win. We cannot stay cloistered away from others forever, attitudes do not change if we are forever separated, but the fear, panic and violence that could spread now and threaten a civil war in our own borders. Even allowing those fleeing into our borders to stay in camps breeds danger. Thoughts of gratitude of escaping horror soon turn to why they are forced to leave in such conditions when others live better and finer lives because of magic and how they must take from those people,"

Drusus sighed.

"What solution have you reached?" Berengar asked.

"None," Cornelius sighed.

"What if instead, you carve out some of the wasteland to the east? Name it a free city under the protection of Magistowe, allow people to flee there, have the Grand Duchess oversee it, have some magic to help settle them, provide basic needs and a basis for building their lives and then let them be. It is not a camp, if people wish to return to their home country, they can, but it keeps those who would be a danger to our community separate from it," Berengar suggested.

Drusus smiled broadly.

"You called it 'our' community."

"I did," Berengar smiled.

"It is a good plan for the temporary dealing with this. I shall put it to the council and perhaps it will help elevate some of the risks for now. But it does not help us with the traitor," Cornelius said with frustration.

"We shall not find that solution tonight, old friend. Come, let us take Berengar to Riley and then rest ourselves. Besides, Prince Cynfael will want to speak with them both come morning," Drusus said.

"Prince Cynfael is here?" Berengar asked with surprise and relief.

"He is. He sought refuge with the Grand Duchess not long ago, that was an interesting turn of events you missed, but he is living in the city now. All shall be revealed soon," Cornelius smiled and looked a great deal more relaxed than he had been.

"Shall we walk or do you want to go directly?" Berengar asked lightly, causing both Drusus and Cornelius to laugh heartily.

"Who would have thought the knight-marshal would take so readily to our lifestyle. Come we shall go directly. I shall take you. Cornelius, to your bed man," Drusus said, taking Berengar's arm. The two men vanished from sight and Cornelius sighed.

He went down to check on the two stable boys, and satisfied they were comfortable, did as Drusus instructed.

Berengar and Drusus reappeared in Riley's home. The four healers were working in the bedroom to heal her but it was clear that they were quickly becoming fatigued.

"My friends, that is all you can do tonight. You must all rest. Berengar shall watch over her. We shall see what her spirit can do to heal her come the morning," Drusus said.

"Very well," one of the healers sighed. There was clear frustration on their faces and it was evident that they could do no more than they had but did not want to admit they could not heal her.

"The council should know she is with child, sir. The babe is healthy, but her own magic protected the child rather than herself. I don't even think she knew to control it in such a fashion, but instinct is a powerful thing," another healer said.

"With child?" Berengar asked with surprise.

"Yes, sir," the healer replied.

"My congratulations to you both," Drusus smiled and hope seemed to kindle behind his eyes. "I suspect that only you will be able to help her heal. I shall tell the others."

"Thank you, all for your work," Berengar said to the healers and each nodded to him in turn before vanishing.

"Do you need me?" Drusus asked.

"No, but thank you. Will you come at first light?" Berengar asked.

"I shall. Until then, be well," Drusus said and disappeared.

Berengar could not help but laugh to himself at the change in Drusus' attitude towards him, but he was glad to have such a friend in the man. He turned his attention to Riley, picking her up from the bed and carrying her across to the hidden entrance to the wellspring.

He laid her unconscious body down beside the fountain of magic and waited.

Chapter 11

The news of Riley's pregnancy spread life wildfire around the cities, towns and settlements of Magistowe. Her return and such great joy that she would bring new life into the world seemed to breathe fresh life into every corner of the country.

Riley rested in the wellspring for three days before she regained her strength and was able to meet with the council.

Each day Drusus had come to visit and speak with Berengar on her condition and to pass on any important news.

The three days it took Riley to rest were the same three days that it took the Grand Duchess and Meridier to travel to the city.

Prince Cynfael came to meet with Berengar and the two were relieved to see the other in such good health. The prince told of Acanthus' campaign against him and the poisoning of the king's mind. He had no one else to turn to he could trust not to hand him over to his father and certain death, save for the Grand Duchess.

Though the assassins had cooled the relations between the pair, she had at least been gracious enough to not return the favour, and instead had offered him sanctuary within the country, but not in her hall.

Drusus had come to collect the Prince and bring him to Magistowe proper, and the pair had soon found that they had a great deal in common. Their time together had forged a friendship that had developed into something more, and the prince had never seemed more free and happy than he was now.

Berengar's suggestion to deal with the refugees was approved by the council, and three small towns around a larger city were created in the eastern wasteland. They were given autonomy to a point and placed under the jurisdiction of the Grand Duchess.

Her authority was respected, on the whole, and though there were some problems, it was the best outcome that anyone could have hoped for.

With Riley pregnant, it was agreed that there should be no direct attack made against the darkness until she had given birth and the child was of an age that they were not reliant upon her for their survival.

The wards and protections around the cities and country and were strengthened as the lands beyond their country fell to war, famine and plague.

Berengar settled into life in Magistowe far quicker than anyone could have predicted. He was one of the few non-magical users in the main city, but he was well respected and often seen in the company of the council members, Prince Cynfael and the scholars who wished to learn more about other nations.

Riley was seen in pubic a handful of times. Her appearance served to keep moods light and bolstered, but despite all of this, the threat of the traitor remained. Small things happened around the city with no explanation for them other than someone or something trying to cause discord and chaos in the city and surrounding area.

Neither magic, nor Berengar's own plans could catch the instigators, and the frustration of it all had Cornelius calling for an inquisition to be formed. This was widely denounced by the other council members, but it meant that Berengar redoubled his efforts.

Six months after their return, Riley went into labour and in the glow of the wellspring, with Berengar beside her, she gave birth to triplets. Three girls, all blessed with her magic.

"These girls will be the ones to carry on your legacy, they will see this land thrive and grow. It will be a place of harmony, learning, and everything that you wanted this to be. But there is yet one thing you must do. One thing that must be down to secure their future and the future of this land," her father said, as he beamed with pride over his three granddaughters.

"And what is that?" Berengar asked.

"Riley must bind the darkness using her own magic and lifeforce to seal it away. It will not stop the darkness entirely but the main host will not be able to harm any. Doing this is the only way to protect this country, your daughters and put an end to the wars and plagues that rage beyond these lands," Godfrey said with a heavy sigh.

"I understand. I will do what I must," Riley agreed, over Berengar's protests.

Nothing Berengar could say would sway the mind of his wife to anything other than her using her own magic and spirit to seal away Acanthus. He made all sorts of plans that would break Acanthus power and hold, but none would stop the darkness.

Riley did not tell the rest of the council of what must be done, and made Berengar to promise not to speak of it either.

The triplets' arrival was celebrated throughout Magistowe and gifts and blessings were heaped upon them. They were given names that both parents agreed upon.

Cintia was the oldest, the first born of the daughters. Her hair and her eyes were both jet black and she was the first to wake every morning and the last to go to sleep.

Inola was the middle child. Her hair was a shock of red and her eyes were green. Her skin was much fairer than that of her sisters, and she had not cried once - not even when she was born.

Alcina was the youngest of the triplets. Her hair was blonde and her eyes were as blue as the wellspring. She was adored by everyone that laid eyes upon her, and was already a favourite of Drusus and the Grand Duchess.

All three girls were loved by their parents and the people they would one day lead. Berengar and Riley would spend hours watching the three girls sleep and then would retire to bed and hold each other silently before they fell asleep.

Riley knew that the time to face Acanthus was

drawing nearer with every passing day and that at some point, they would need to establish when that would be. Her father was still able to reach out from beyond the veil using the wellspring, but her mother's magic had long faded from this world.

Riley knew it was because Adele had used so much of her power battling the darkness that had defeated both her parents. She wondered if she died fighting Acanthus whether she would have enough magic left to appear in the wellspring too.

These were thoughts that she never voiced aloud, and never shared with Berengar. Neither of them talked about how long they had left before they had to turn their thoughts to battling Acanthus, but they both knew that it would be sooner than either of them would wish.

CHAPTER 12

"Three years," Grand Duchess Tempest said firmly to Riley. The council had been assembled and Riley and Berengar had finally divulged what had to be done to deal with the darkness.

The news had not been greeted with any form of enthusiasm. Cornelius had completely refused to accept the plan and was now desperately searching for an alternative with Leader and Hellebore.

Prince Cynfael and Sandulf, the partner of the Grand Duchess, had both been granted approval to sit with the council whilst they discussed Acanthus and what was to be done. The prince, Drusus, Sandulf, Mairi, Natrix, and Rowena had all been dumbfounded by the news and had yet to find any words to contribute to the discussion.

Meridier had whispered with Tempest for a moment before the grand duchess had spoken. All eyes had turned abruptly towards her.

"What do you mean, three years?" Hellebore asked slowly.

"Three years is how long the triplets will need their mother. They have no concept of time or death before that age. Should this prove to be the suicidal mission that we all suspect, then it must wait until the girls can survive and understand the loss of their mother," Tempest said calmly.

"Only three years?" Berengar asked with wide eyes.

"The girls will need her much longer than that, they have much to learn about this world, their powers, and their heritage, it must be longer, at least twenty years," Cornelius protested.

"Do not be a fool, old man," Meridier snapped. "This land cannot hope to survive for twenty years with the darkness gaining power in such an unchecked manner. We must act sooner, rather than later. We cannot wait twenty years."

"And how will they learn? We cannot teach them!" Rowena finally spoke.

"No, you can't. But I learned without your help, and they shall as well," Riley sighed.

"So you agree? Three years?" Drusus asked sadly.

"I do," Riley sighed. "It means not only do I have three years with my daughters, but we have three years to find out how to defeat Acanthus and find the traitor."

"We have failed to find the traitor so far, what makes you think that we shall find them now?" Mairi asked with an edge of frustration to her voice.

"Because we shall draw out the traitor and Acanthus with the wellspring," Riley replied with a slight smile curling at the corner of her mouth.

"You would risk the wellspring?" Leander asked, dumbfounded.

"No, but we can use the wellspring to draw both the traitor and Acanthus into a trap," Riley said.

Silence fell on the room as the council considered what was being proposed.

"I second the idea," Natrix said with good humour. "We kill two birds with one stone."

"And what if the traitor hears of this trap and helps Acanthus avoid it?" Sandulf asked.

"He will hear of the trap for certain, but he will not be able to resist it," Riley said firmly.

"Do you know who the traitor is?" Cornelius asked with a frown.

"I believe so. He is the only person it makes sense for it to be, and I suspect that you have not considered him a threat that needs to be interrogated," Riley replied, shaking her head.

"Who have we not looked at that would know such vital -" Tempest's voice trailed off and her hand flew to her mouth. "You cannot mean -"

"I do," Riley said.

"Host," Meridier said with annoyance and slammed her fist down on the arm of her chair.

Cornelius and Berengar both closed their eyes as they both realised that Riley was right.

"We did not suspect him at all, nor was he questioned in the circle. He has had access to all that passes between us as Tempest's second and has done everything to show his loyalty without arousing suspicion," Cornelius sighed.

"We should deal with him now," Drusus said leaping to his feet.

"No," Prince Cynfael said. "Riley is right. We need to use him to trap Acanthus, but that does not mean that we cannot trap Host first."

"You think Acanthus would listen to him if we show our hand now?" Berengar asked with a raised eyebrow.

"He won't be able to risk not listening to him. We shall give him whatever information Riley deems to be necessary, let him believe the wellspring has been uncovered and Host was caught there, which led to his capture and punishment, only for him to escape to report to Acanthus," Leander reasoned.

"We keep him as a prisoner until we are ready for Acanthus to know. But we cannot do this now, it will be too long between the capture and escape to be credible," Mairi argued.

"So for now, we do not show Host we know. He can be sent to oversee the towns and cities in the east for Tempest, let him build his own block of power that he believes is strengthening his position, but we surround him with those we know can be trusted and are able to serve him and provide the information we want him to hear, then betray him at the appointed hour. He will not have the access to the council he once had, but he will still be useful to Acanthus," Natrix reasoned.

"Then we shall do this at once. Rowena and I can select those who will serve as his counsel and advisers there," Tempest agreed.

"The rest of us shall begin to lay the trap for Acanthus and prepare for the worst," Hellebore said with a melancholy edged to their voice.

"Are you sure this is the best course of action?" Mairi asked Riley one final time.

"Yes," Riley replied.

"Very well, then let us be about our work," Cornelius sighed.

Three years passed all too quickly. Cintia, Inola, and Alcina grew in grace and all greatly resembled their mother. They learned to walk and talk and showed signs of the magic that they had inherited from their mother.

Plans were laid for the trap for Acanthus and when the time was right, Drusus and Prince Cynfael were given guardianship of the three girls, should the battle with Acanthus go badly. Tempest had laid plans to get them out of the city and to a land far across the sea should they need to escape and the other members of the council had been detailed to defensive positions around the city and surrounding lands to battle the darkness and hold it at bay for as long as possible should Riley and Berengar fall.

Riley and Berengar waited deep under the foundations of Magistowe, waiting for Acanthus to come for the wellspring.

Host's capture and escape had all gone to plan and Natrix and Drusus had thoroughly interrogated the traitor until he had given up all those that had helped him willingly and under duress. What would happen to those who had betrayed Magistowe was yet to be determined, but Cornelius was ready to rain down vengeance without prejudice or mercy.

Three days had passed since Host's escape and the hour for the final battle was drawing near. Berengar was ready to leave the wellspring chamber to check on their children when the darkness arrived.

He came without fanfare, like a thief trying to steal into the heart of a great treasure horde. He seemed surprised to find Riley and Berengar waiting for him, but his surprise soon passed.

"You were expecting me, I see," Acanthus

smiled. "I could no more surprise you, than you did me when you came to call. I suppose that is only fair."

"Your informant was swift," Berengar growled in reply.

"Yes, though it seems that he was mistaken in his assertion. This is no more the wellspring than a horse is a human. I commend you for your creative abilities, Riley. You have done great work to make it appear as though this is the wellspring. But only a fool would believe that it is such," Acanthus laughed.

"Then you should not have chosen a fool for an ally," Berengar retorted.

"Indeed, but I do feel it is close. So excuse me," Acanthus said and attempted to leave the cavern. When he failed to use his magic to portal his way out of the cavern, he tried to walk out.

"Is there a problem?" Berengar asked smugly.

"I see you placed wards around this place. How clever, but wards can be broken. You cannot hold me in here by wards alone," Acanthus sneered.

"It is not by words alone that you shall be held here," Riley said. "Ex vi fontis. Pro conservatione vitae. Statera huic mundo et tyrannidi finem imponere, hic te obligamus. In virtute nominis mei."

Acanthus cried out in pain as the ground rose up and seized hold of his limbs. The earthern bonds dragged him across the cavern's floor to the centre of the cavern where a gold circle glowed brightly. As he was thrust into the centre of the circle, the ground returned to it's normal state around the circle.

"This is a pathetic attempt to hold me. You shall regret trifling with me, just as your parents did," Acanthus snarled.

"It is time, Berengar," Riley said. Berengar rushed to her side and held her tightly before he kissed her passionately.

"A virtute nominis eius," Berengar said as Riley reached out her hand so that her fingers brushed the golden light of the circle. "Caitriona."

At the sound of her real name, the first magic

began to pour out of Riley's body in an unstoppable torrent. It whirled around the room before it collided with the golden circle and began to engulf Acanthus' body.

"You witch!" he snarled as he tried desperately to free himself from the magic, but Riley could not hear him. Her body was crumbling in Berengar's arms as her magic and her lifeforce left her. There was nothing Berengar could do to stop what was happening to her and nothing more he could do to protect her.

Acanthus screamed hysterically as he realised what was happening to him and was only silenced when he was completely engulfed by the magic and the golden light faded.

All that remained of Acanthus and Riley was a stone pillar of frozen swirling magic.

Berengar collapsed to his knees and wept unreservedly for what seemed like hours. When he was able to compose himself enough, he made his way slowly out of the cave.

Outside the entrance, Leander, Natrix and Mairi were waiting for him.

"It is done. She is gone," Berengar managed to choke. "Seal it."

The three mages nodded and did as they were bade. There was nothing that they could say to comfort Berengar and they went about their work silently as they grieved for their lost friend.

With Acanthus defeated and sealed away, the plague that had gripped the lands was ended, the paranoia that had gripped King Ruettigur's mind was gone, and the threat of war was gone.

Prince Cynfael became the adjutant of the border towns and cities, that continued to grow under his wise and compassionate rule.

Berengar took Riley's place on the council and led Magistowe until his daughters were ready to assume the mantle of their mother. The girls were raised within the walls of the school where they learned about the different forms of magic in the world as well as the basic education that Berengar believed that everyone should receive.

He could not return to the home he had shared with Riley and instead Natrix took up residence there not only to guard the wellspring, but allow his quarters in the school to be given to Riley's family.

On their 16th birthday, their father brought them to the true wellspring, where Riley Caitriona Sonen, heroine of Magistowe, was waiting to greet her daughters from the fountain of the wellspring and teach them how to use their powers.

AUTHOR'S NOTE

Thanks so much for reading this novella. This originally started as a small project that was to be around 5,000 words to help a man who was about to lose his home. As you can tell, it did not end up as 5,000 words, but in writing this story, it became very apparent that there was a lot more to this story to tell, a lot more to explore, and some amazing characters that I as the author wanted to get to know better, and I am sure you share that sentiment as readers.

Because of this, later this year I will be writing a special edition trilogy that will expand this story and fill out all the details that you want to know - feature Meridier and the mythical creatures, take you to the Grand Duchess Tempest's lands and reveal what happened with the assassins, and show you what happened to the two stable boys as they adjusted to their new lives in Magistowe to name but a few of the details. I hope that this news is exciting and that you look forward to the special edition. These will be done through Kickstarter and then sold direct as there will be a limited run of these books done.

To keep up-to-date on this and other stories from this world, join my ream community for free! - https://reamstories.com/amandahuxley simply click follow under the subscriptions to follow for free and get all the latest news! I am still building this community and the page but I look forward to seeing you there.